Counting the Kisses

Counting the Billions, Volume 3

Lexy Timms

Published by Dark Shadow Publishing, 2018.

COUNTING THE KISSES

First edition. November 19, 2018.

Written by Lexy Timms.

Also by Lexy Timms

A Burning Love Series
Spark of Passion
Flame of Desire
Blaze of Ecstasy

A Chance at Forever Series
Forever Perfect
Forever Desired
Forever Together

BBW Romance Series
Capturing Her Beauty
Pursuing Her Dreams
Tracing Her Curves

Beating the Biker Series
Making Her His
Making the Break

Making of Them

Billionaire Banker Series

Banking on Him

Price of Passion

Investing in Love

Knowing Your Worth

Treasured Forever

Billionaire Holiday Romance Series

Driving Home for Christmas

The Valentine Getaway

Cruising Love

Billionaire in Disguise Series

Facade

Illusion

Charade

Billionaire Secrets Series

The Secret

Freedom

Courage

Trust

Impulse

Billionaire Secrets Box Set Books #1-3

Building Billions
Building Billions - Part 1
Building Billions - Part 2
Building Billions - Part 3

Conquering Warrior Series
Ruthless

Counting the Billions
Counting the Days
Counting On You
Counting the Kisses

Diamond in the Rough Anthology
Billionaire Rock
Billionaire Rock - part 2

Dominating PA Series
Her Personal Assistant - Part 1
Her Personal Assistant Box Set

Fake Billionaire Series
Faking It

Temporary CEO
Caught in the Act
Never Tell A Lie
Fake Christmas

Firehouse Romance Series
Caught in Flames
Burning With Desire
Craving the Heat
Firehouse Romance Complete Collection

For His Pleasure
Elizabeth
Georgia
Madison

Fortune Riders MC Series
Billionaire Biker
Billionaire Ransom
Billionaire Misery

Fragile Series
Fragile Touch
Fragile Kiss
Fragile Love

Hades' Spawn Motorcycle Club

One You Can't Forget

One That Got Away

One That Came Back

One You Never Leave

One Christmas Night

Hades' Spawn MC Complete Series

Hard Rocked Series

Rhyme

Harmony

Lyrics

Heart of Stone Series

The Protector

The Guardian

The Warrior

Heart of the Battle Series

Celtic Viking

Celtic Rune

Celtic Mann

Heart of the Battle Series Box Set

Heistdom Series
Master Thief
Goldmine
Diamond Heist
Smile For Me

Just About Series
About Love
About Truth
About Forever

Justice Series
Seeking Justice
Finding Justice
Chasing Justice
Pursuing Justice
Justice - Complete Series

Kissed by the Billionaire Series
Kissed by Passion

Love You Series
Love Life
Need Love

My Love

Managing the Billionaire

Never Enough

Managing the Bosses Series

The Boss

The Boss Too

Who's the Boss Now

Love the Boss

I Do the Boss

Wife to the Boss

Employed by the Boss

Brother to the Boss

Senior Advisor to the Boss

Forever the Boss

Christmas With the Boss

Billionaire in Control

Billionaire Makes Millions

Gift for the Boss - Novella 3.5

Managing the Bosses Box Set #1-3

Model Mayhem Series

Shameless

Modesty

Imperfection

Moment in Time

Highlander's Bride

Victorian Bride

Modern Day Bride

A Royal Bride

Forever the Bride

Outside the Octagon

Submit

Protecting Diana Series

Her Bodyguard

Her Defender

Her Champion

Her Protector

Her Forever

Protecting Layla Series

His Mission

His Objective

His Devotion

Racing Hearts Series

Rush

Pace
Fast

Reverse Harem Series
Primals
Archaic
Unitary

RIP Series
Track the Ripper
Hunt the Ripper
Pursue the Ripper

R&S Rich and Single Series
Alex Reid
Parker

Saving Forever
Saving Forever - Part 1
Saving Forever - Part 2
Saving Forever - Part 3
Saving Forever - Part 4
Saving Forever - Part 5
Saving Forever - Part 6
Saving Forever Part 7
Saving Forever - Part 8

Saving Forever Boxset Books #1-3

Shifting Desires Series

Jungle Heat

Jungle Fever

Jungle Blaze

Southern Romance Series

Little Love Affair

Siege of the Heart

Freedom Forever

Soldier's Fortune

Spelling Love Series

The Author

The Book Boyfriend

The Words of Love

Tattooist Series

Confession of a Tattooist

Surrender of a Tattooist

Heart of a Tattooist

Hopes & Dreams of a Tattooist

Tennessee Romance
Whisky Lullaby
Whisky Melody
Whisky Harmony

The Bad Boy Alpha Club
Battle Lines - Part 1
Battle Lines

The Brush Of Love Series
Every Night
Every Day
Every Time
Every Way
Every Touch

The Debt
The Debt: Part 1 - Damn Horse
The Debt: Complete Collection

The University of Gatica Series
The Recruiting Trip
Faster
Higher

Stronger
Dominate
No Rush
University of Gatica - The Complete Series

T.N.T. Series
Troubled Nate Thomas - Part 1
Troubled Nate Thomas - Part 2
Troubled Nate Thomas - Part 3

Undercover Series
Perfect For Me
Perfect For You
Perfect For Us

Unknown Identity Series
Unknown
Unpublished
Unexposed
Unsure
Unwritten
Unknown Identity Box Set: Books #1-3

Unlucky Series
Unlucky in Love
UnWanted

UnLoved Forever

Wet & Wild Series

Stormy Love

Savage Love

Secure Love

Worth It Series

Worth Billions

Worth Every Cent

Worth More Than Money

You & Me - A Bad Boy Romance

Just Me

Touch Me

Kiss Me

Standalone

Wash

Loving Charity

Summer Lovin'

Love & College

Billionaire Heart

First Love

Frisky and Fun Romance Box Collection

Beating Hades' Bikers

Watch for more at www.lexytimms.com.

Counting The Billions Book 3

COUNTING The Kisses

USA TODAY BESTSELLING AUTHOR

LEXY TIMMS

Counting the Kisses

Counting the Billions Series #3

Cover by: Book Cover by Design[1]

1. **http://bookcoverbydesign.co.uk/**

Counting the Billions Series

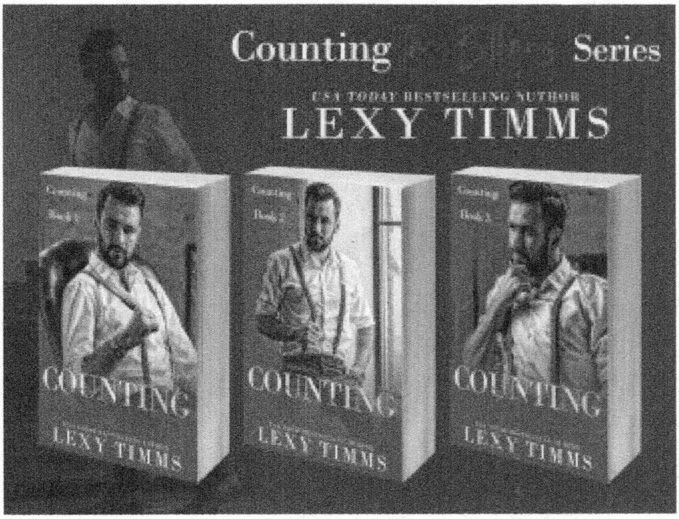

Book 1 – Counting the Days
Book 2 – Counting on You
Book 3 – Counting the Kisses

Find Lexy Timms:

LEXY TIMMS NEWSLETTER:

http://eepurl.com/9i0vD

Lexy Timms Facebook Page:

https://www.facebook.com/SavingForever

Lexy Timms Website:

http://www.lexytimms.com

Counting
Book 3
COUNTING
LEXY TIMMS

Want to read more...
For **FREE**?
Sign up for Lexy Timms' newsletter
And she'll send you updates on new releases, ARC copies of books and a whole lotta fun!
Sign up for news and updates!
http://eepurl.com/9i0vD

Counting The Kisses Blurb

"HE ASKED ME WHAT MY favorite position was. I said CEO."

Daniel and I have been through so much already. But now there's this trial on top of everything else.

And it's not just the court trial for Daniel. It's also a trial run of me as temporary CEO of his company.

If things end badly, I'll be forced to recognize just how tricky mixing business with pleasure can be.

Because problems at work don't just stay at work.

Is there any way for Daniel and I to fix our relationship again? Or is this the end of us for good this time?

Counting
Book 3
COUNTING
USA TODAY BESTSELLING AUTHOR
LEXY TIMMS

Chapter 1

Daniel

There was no good way to tell Abby.

All day, I'd been trying to figure out some way to broach the subject with her, to tell her that Gerrard was taking me to court for assault. But I just didn't want to lose this.

This, right now, being dinner with her at my house. She smiled across the table at me as she took a sip of her wine. "What are you thinking about?" she asked. "You've been quiet all evening."

I shook my head, but I couldn't think of any way to respond to that. It was now or never. I slowly reached over to the side table and grabbed the envelope full of documents. Then, just as carefully, I slid it across the table toward her.

Abby frowned at me and then lifted the envelope, sliding the documents out of it. I watched her emotions flicker across her face as she read through them. First, there was shock. Then, grim acceptance of it. I wondered what was going through her mind right now. I knew that fight had been part of what screwed things up between us the first time. Things had been going great, but she hadn't liked the anger she'd seen burst out of me that night, with that stupid confrontation.

I hadn't been able to help it. Gerrard had told Abby that basically the only reason I had hired her was so that I could sleep with her. That I would fire her as soon as I was done with her. And not only that, but he had said I had done that before with other women in the office. The worst part, though, was definitely the look on Abby's face when he told her all of this. That hurt and surprise. The resigned look she got as though she should have expected that all along.

I hadn't been able to handle it. And in retrospect, what I should have done was just steer Abby out of there, take her away from Gerrard and his lies, make sure that she understood the truth.

I hadn't hired her for her looks. No, she was amazing at her job, and I had realized she would be, right from the start of the interview. She was smart and she was witty, and she did her research. She was thorough.

Sure, I was attracted to her. But that wasn't why I had hired her.

Beyond that, she wasn't just some fling to me. Even then, even though our relationship had been pretty new at the time, I knew that she was special to me. I thought that she would know that, and it hurt to realize that she really thought Gerrard was telling her the truth.

Another reason to punch Gerrard. But now, it was the biggest regret of my life.

Abby finally looked up at me, sliding the papers back across the table towards me. She didn't say a word, and I could tell from the way that she was looking at me that she was expecting me to say something. I fumbled for the words.

"I don't want to open this can of worms again any more than you do," I finally managed to say, my voice grim. "If I could go back and make it so that night never happened, believe me, I would do it in an heartbeat."

"But you can't," Abby said flatly. She shrugged, looking unhappy. "I hate to say it, but you do deserve to face the consequences for your actions."

"I never said I didn't." I sighed. "And I am sorry for what I did. I hope you realize that. I completely overreacted. But I have to admit that if I were to go back and do that night all over again, I probably would do things exactly the same way. I just couldn't stand the way he was talking to you, as though you were just trash. As though you were nothing at all to me. He had no right to talk to you that way, and I believe in standing up for the people I care about."

"I know you do," Abby said quietly, much to my surprise. She sighed. "So what does this mean? How are you going to juggle this on top of everything else?"

"I don't really know," I admitted. "I've never been to court before. I do have a feeling that things are probably going to get messy once the media catches wind of what's happening." I paused. "I'm already thinking that I'll have to take some time off work. This is going to eat up a lot of my time, I'm sure, plus I don't exactly want to drag the company's reputation through the mud with me. Better that the company keep moving along in the background as much as it can."

"Right," Abby said, nodding.

That was one of the things I had been thinking about all afternoon. Who could I possibly put in charge of McGregor Enterprises while I was fighting this court case? The only person really qualified to step in for me was Abby. And I knew that she had dreams of one day becoming CEO of a company. She was definitely bright enough, and I trusted her to make all the right decisions for the company.

The trouble was that she was still so new to working for me. If she had been there for even a year, it would have been different. She would have known all the major players, and more importantly, they all would have known her. But as things stood, I wasn't sure if reactions would be particularly favorable to her taking over the company right now, and I didn't want her to get frustrated by stodgy old men refusing to do business with her like they would with me, all because they had misperceptions of her business acumen due to her gender.

Not only that, but I knew she wasn't keen on being right in the middle of a media maelstrom. There had already been so much press about our relationship in the short amount of time since we had gone public that I knew this trial would be tricky enough as it was. Put her in charge of the business while I was off at a trial facing assault charges over something Gerrard had said to her? That was a recipe for a media shitstorm the likes of which I wasn't even sure that I could handle, and I had a lot more experience with taking crap from the media.

The trouble was, no matter how I wracked my brain, I couldn't think of any other way to do things. I didn't want to bring in an outsider. And Abby was the only one I could trust to run the business the way I would.

I couldn't spring that on her, though, until I knew how she felt about this whole situation.

So for now, I left the question open and told her I was thinking of taking a temporary leave of absence and putting someone in charge of the business. Abby, thankfully, didn't question it. She was probably thinking along the same lines as me.

I cleared my throat. "I'd understand if you want to cool things off until things settle down for me again," I said, because I had to tell her that. It felt like things had just finally gotten good between us, and now this. It broke my heart to think of her walking out of my life over this, but at the same time, it was like she had said: I deserved to face the consequences of my actions. I might not like them, but at the end of the day, what kind of a man would I be if I ran away from them?

Abby frowned at me, and I could tell that she was carefully considering her words. "I'm still not happy that you resorted to violence," she said finally. "But I do understand that you were just trying to protect me. And I also know you better now. You're not just a violent guy. You're impulsive sometimes, but I guess I had to know that you were before we ever started this; it's what makes you so good at business and fearless in your decisions." She gave me a half smile.

But I shook my head at her. "That's not the only reason to cool things off," I reminded her. "The media is going to have a field day. They're going to want to know what you think about all of this. If you're okay with what I did. There could be some terrible stories about me. Or about us. I just don't even know where they'll start on this one."

"They're going to write those stories either way," Abby pointed out. "We've already gone public about our relationship. I think it would only lead to more snide remarks if we appeared to break it off because of the trial."

I grimaced, unable to meet her eyes. "You're probably right," I admitted. "If there was any way for me to make it so that you weren't involved, trust me, I would do it. Still, I don't want you to feel like you have to be there for me through this. To support me."

"Are you trying to make me break up with you?" Abby asked, sounding confused. Before I could answer, she was standing up and coming around the table to me, taking both of my hands in hers. "Daniel, I can't tell you that you didn't do anything wrong. I also can't tell you that I'm happy to be caught up in the middle of all of this. But we're here now." She paused. "Relationships are never going to be easy. There are always going to be difficult things to work through."

"I know that," I said. She cut me off with a finger to my lips before I could continue.

"Daniel, I'm here for you through this," Abby said quietly, looking seriously into my eyes. "Whatever you need. I'm sticking by your side. The media can say what they want about it."

I exhaled a breath I hadn't realized I had been holding. "I'm glad to hear that," I told her. Then, even more slowly: "I have a proposition for you."

Chapter 2

Abby

I HAD TOLD DANIEL THE truth: I wasn't exactly happy to be caught in the middle of all this drama. Life had been so much simpler before I first went to work for him, that was for sure.

Maybe I should stop and think about all of this. Decide if there was a better way to handle things. But the only thing I could think of that would get me out of the picture would be for me really to get out of the picture. To quit working for him, break off our relationship, and start over somewhere new. Even then, there was bound to be some ugly media coverage, people saying things that they had no right to be saying about me.

And really, what kind of example did that set for Zach and Layla? If I truly believed that Daniel deserved to face the consequences of his actions, then I had to realize that I deserved to face the consequences of my own actions as well. I might not have intended to end up in such a soap opera, but this was where my choices had led me.

To be honest, what really sealed my position as being firmly on Daniel's side was just how torn up he seemed telling me about this. I truly believed that if he could somehow change things, if he could protect me from the media scrutiny, then he would do it. In a heartbeat. You couldn't fault a guy for that.

No, Daniel was a good guy. All the time that I had spent with him had only further emphasized what a good guy he was. He wasn't perfect, no. No one was, though. But he wasn't nearly the jerk of a playboy that the media made him out to be. If my being there at his side helped his cause in any way, then I wanted to be there.

Not least of which because I loved him and I didn't want to lose him over this, whatever my feelings on all the drama really were.

Now, though, I narrowed my eyes at him. "What kind of a proposition?" I asked warily. I wanted to support him through this, but in light of how carefully he had orchestrated our public announcement of our relationship, I was worried. Did he want the two of us to do an interview or something, letting the public know about the assault charges prior to the news leaking out in some other way?

I wanted to support him, and I wanted to be there at his side, but I wasn't sure I was comfortable sitting through an interview with him.

Daniel grinned at me, though. "Remember when I asked you what your favorite position is?"

I stared blankly at him for a moment. My favorite position? Was he planning on rewarding me for sticking with him by giving me mind-blowing sex? The very thought of that made me feel cheap, somehow. But I also couldn't remember ever having a conversation like that with him. We were still new to exploring each other's bodies and preferences, but we hadn't really had to sit down and talk about them. We seemed to innately understand one another better than that, even from the first time.

Daniel was still grinning at me, though. "You said CEO," he said, and I realized he had been joking.

I snorted out a laugh and shook my head. "You're terrible," I told him.

"I know," Daniel said, looking pleased at having lightened the conversation a little. But his eyes were still serious. "When I first interviewed you for the advisory job, you said that you wanted to be a CEO one day."

I nodded. I remembered. But for the life of me I couldn't figure out where he was going with this.

"Like I said before, I'm probably going to have to step away from work for a little bit, until all of this blows over. I just don't have the time to devote to the business right now, and on top of that, I've worked hard to build up my business. I don't want that strong foundation jeopardized now because clients don't want to do business with someone who's in court fighting assault charges." He looked pained as he said that, and I wished there was something that I could say to reassure him that his business partners weren't the type of guys to care about idle gossip.

But this wasn't just gossip. Daniel really had punched Gerrard, and the assault charges were legitimate.

Daniel didn't dwell on it, either way. Instead, he dropped a bombshell: "I'd like you to stand in for me as Interim CEO of McGregor Enterprises while I deal with Gerrard."

I gaped at him. "What?" I asked in shock. "You want me to run your company?" My mind was whirling as I thought of the possibility of it all. McGregor Enterprises was no small company. I knew a lot about its day-to-day operations already, and I had joined Daniel in a ton of meetings with various business associates. But that didn't mean I was ready to run the company in his absence. Even if I was able to ask him questions as needed, the risk was too high. I could make a decision that would undo years of work he had put into things.

Not only that, but I was just so new to the company. I was still trying to learn from Daniel. I was still trying to grasp some of the decisions he made. There had to be someone who was more qualified than me.

"You're the best choice," Daniel told me.

"That can't be true," I said, shaking my head. "Some of the other guys have been with the company since your father was running it. I'm sure they know ten times what I know about things."

"They know the business, sure," Daniel said, nodding gravely. "But you're the only one I trust to head the company in my stead. You do business like I do. And you see things the way that I do. The other employees will all be there to answer any questions that you have. Actually, I was talking with Erin this afternoon about putting together some files with all the information about our shareholders and such so that you have some solid reference material for any decisions you need to make." He paused. "But you're good at reading people, and you make smart business choices."

I was flattered by his words, I had to admit, but I still found myself shaking my head. "Daniel, you know the shareholders aren't going to support something like that. Plus, the media would be all over it."

"I know." Daniel sighed, looking away from me. I could see the unhappy pinch at the corners of his lips. "However, you're the only person I can trust to run the company in my stead. But if you don't want to do it, I understand. And please, don't feel like there's any pressure from me. I know this would affect your career just as much as my company. I just want you to think about it, that's all. The trial starts in two days, on Thursday, so there's not that much time to sort things out, but this isn't your mess. I'm the one who has to deal with it."

I could see how worried he was, and I knew exactly who his worry was for. He wasn't thinking about himself at that moment; he was thinking about the company. He was thinking about the employees that had been with him for years, and the employees that had been with the company even before he had taken it over upon his father's death. I knew he cared about each and every one of them.

I wished I could tell him that yes; I would take over the reins while he fought this legal battle with Gerrard. But I knew I needed to think things through first. If nothing else, a hasty decision like this wasn't a good first move to make as interim CEO of the company. "I need to sleep on it at least," I told Daniel, and he nodded his understanding.

"Definitely take some time and think about it," he agreed. "I totally understand that you need to do that." He paused and then added, "But I wouldn't ask if I wasn't confident you could do it. Just let that be part of your thinking about it: there's not a doubt in my mind that you could handle it."

I shook my head, but I couldn't help the small smile that formed on my face. I sank down into his lap, wrapping my arms around him in a quick hug. "That makes one of us," I told him. "I just wish I could be so certain."

"I didn't say that it wouldn't be difficult," Daniel cautioned. "But hey, didn't someone say that relationships were never without their difficulties? Life and business are kind of like that as well, isn't it?"

I laughed and shook my head. "All right, smart-ass," I said, but I couldn't keep the fondness out of my voice. I reached out and brushed my fingers through his hair. "You still want me to stay over tonight, or should I head home and let you get started on preparing your defense?"

Daniel's arms tightened around me. "Stay. Please," he said. He made a face. "You're right that the mature thing to do would probably be to get started on my case right away, but I'd rather not think about this anymore tonight. Things were going so well between us, and now, well."

I gave him a light, chaste kiss. "Things are still going well between us," I promised him. It was another thing I wished I could be a hundred percent sure on. But I knew I didn't want to break up with him over this. I wanted to try to work through things if we could. Maybe it would prove to be too much for this fledgling relationship of ours, but if he was willing to give it a shot, if he was willing to trust me even as far as letting me take over as CEO of his company temporarily, then I was willing to trust him and to take a shot as well.

We'd get through this. I really wanted to believe that.

Again, I thought about those three words, *I love you.* I wanted to say them now, to reassure him that I was going to be there for him no matter what, for as long as I could help it. But at the same time, I didn't want to taint the first time I said those words with the specter of a court case looming over us. The timing now just wasn't what I would have hoped for. So I continued to hold them in reserve. Another time; I would tell him some other time.

Daniel, heedless of my inner turmoil, no doubt caught up in thoughts of his own, scooped me up into his arms and carried me up to his bedroom. We were both silent the entire way, and neither of us spoke as we stripped off our clothing and slipped into bed side by side.

I couldn't seem to even close my eyes, though. My mind was spinning, thoughts going a mile a minute. I really did want to be a CEO one day. But I had never even imagined that day might come so soon. Sure, it was just a temporary position until this whole thing with Gerrard was over and done with. But it was still a pretty big deal.

I didn't think I was ready for things to change so much. And what's more, I didn't want things to change so much, not so soon. Things were already so different now from how they'd been before I had gone to work for McGregor Enterprises. I wasn't ready for more change already.

Like Daniel had said, things had just really started to seem good between the two of us. Things had finally settled down, and we were finding our rhythm. And now it was all thrown off again. Could I keep doing this? Could I continue to let the drama change my life every time I turned around?

But on the other hand, could I quit doing this? Leave Daniel and leave a position that I loved, all because I was too scared or inflexible to change? That seemed just as out of the question.

I just didn't know what to do, and unfortunately, I was no closer to thinking up any solutions by the time I finally drifted off to sleep.

Chapter 3

Daniel

I SHUFFLED ANOTHER set of papers together and looked around, grimacing when I saw how much information was scattered around the office. I was trying to get everything ready to hand control of the company over to Abby, but I just didn't know what she might need, and trying to anticipate all possible occurrences was proving challenging. It would be easier to come up with a better organizational system, I was sure, if Abby were there helping me. But she still hadn't given me an answer as to whether or not she was willing to take over as temporary CEO, and I didn't want her to feel any sort of pressure over it.

That said, I didn't have any time to waste. The trial started the next day, and although I really did want to get this over with sooner rather than later, at the same time, the pressure was on. If it wasn't Abby taking over for me while I was gone, well. Someone was going to have to step up to the plate.

Another thing that I hadn't talked to Abby about: I had discussed things with a few of the guys I did business with. I had a backup guy in mind, an old friend of mine who usually built startups and sold them off. He was in between projects right now, and he had the time to take over for me. I wasn't sure that I really trusted him with my company because I knew he was a lot more cutthroat in business than I usually was.

No, he wouldn't be my first choice. But again, I was trying to prepare for all possibilities here.

I was pretty sure it wouldn't come to that, though. Abby hadn't given me an answer yet, and I knew there was a lot for her to think over.

But I was pretty confident that she would rise to the challenge. She was the kind of woman who liked a challenge in her life, though, and I knew she wanted to be a CEO eventually anyway. What better way to learn than to try her hand at this now? The learning curve might be a little steep, but I hadn't lied when I told her that I was completely certain that she could do this.

I glanced impatiently at my watch. Abby was at lunch with her best friend and sister-in-law, Leanne, now. I strongly suspected that she would come back with an answer one way or the other. As certain as I was that she was going to agree to take over for me, there was still the slight chance that she would decide not to. And by now, I just wanted to know one way or another. There was too much else that was up in the air about this trial, and I honestly just wanted one thing sorted out.

Erin knocked on my door, poking her head into the office. "Hey, boss, how's it going?" she asked. I could see the sympathy in her eyes; she'd been my assistant for long enough to know all the chaos that my job really entailed. She looked around at the piles of papers and shook her head, a grin on her lips. "Abby's going to have her work cut out for her. The first thing to do will be sorting through all of this!"

I grimaced. "I just feel like I have to prepare her for anything that could happen," I said.

"Has she agreed to take over for now?" Erin asked curiously.

"Not yet," I said. "I'm expecting an answer when she gets back from lunch. I think she's discussing things with her sister-in-law as we speak."

Erin nodded sagely. "Well, whoever steps in for you, I think you've given them access to the total archives of the business, from the look of things. In paper form, no less." I gave her a look, and she laughed, holding up both hands. "Relax," she said. "I'm sure things will be fine. Even without the stacks and stacks of research you've compiled."

I sighed. "Just be as helpful to Abby as you can. That's all I ask. She's probably going to be nervous, and she'll need a sounding board and someone to hold her hand if necessary. You've been with this business for longer than she has, and you know things that no one else in this company does."

"Sure thing," Erin said easily. We'd already had this conversation but I couldn't help reiterate the thought. It made me feel better to have her assure me again that she'd be there for Abby as needed.

"I'll do my best to be there for her," I said, promising that to Erin as much as myself. And as much as to Abby, although she wasn't there to hear it. "I just have no clue how messy this thing with Gerrard could get."

"I'll do everything I can to help her," Erin said again.

"Thanks," I said gratefully.

"Good luck to you," Erin added. "But I know everything will work out. Gerrard's just being an ass because he knows you have money and because he knows that the media loves a story like this." She shrugged. "But we're all rooting for you."

I sighed and shook my head. "Thanks," I said, watching as she left. Then, I sank back into the seat behind my desk, pressing my fingertips against my eyelids, feeling the start of a migraine brewing behind my eyes.

She was right, Gerrard was just being an ass. I was still shocked that things had gone so wrong with him. He had been my trusted advisor for years, and he had worked for the company for more than two decades. I never would have suspected that he would start selling stories about me to the media, or that he would start giving them tip-offs as to my location or upcoming business decisions. I was still reeling from that betrayal.

And now, this. It was like he just couldn't get enough of tormenting me. It made me wonder what the hell I had done to get on his bad side. But it wasn't like I could just ask him that.

Maybe it really was all about the money. I had thought that I was paying him a fair salary, but maybe it just wasn't enough.

I shook my head again, trying to forget those thoughts. It didn't matter if Gerrard was just being an ass; I still had to go through this trial and everything that came with it.

I couldn't help feeling a bit worried. Unfortunately, people like Gerrard just seemed to have a way of finding me, and of taking advantage of me. Because although I might think that he was just an ass, I knew that the underdog—Gerrard in this case—usually had the support of the public.

The trial would be tricky. I had beat up Gerrard; that was a fact. After publically firing him, no less. And I knew that no one really believed that I had hired Abby for her brains and business acumen. No, they were all sure that the media had it right, that I was just looking for someone to fuck. So they would believe Gerrard when he said he had been wrongly fired, that I had only ousted him so I could put a young, leggy blonde in his place.

My hands clenched into fists. It was all lies, but then again, most of what the press had been publishing about me for years now was lies, or at least heavily embellished truths and speculations. The public always ate it up before; there was no reason to think that things would be any different this time around. My lawyer had already run through the possible outcomes of this trial with me, and I had to admit, it had me worried.

But what had me most worried was that somehow Abby would decide it was all too much for her and leave me. I didn't know what I would do if that happened.

Chapter 4

Abby

I SMILED OVER AT LEANNE as our soup and sandwiches were delivered to the table. "Thank you again for meeting me," I told her, hoping she couldn't see just how weak my smile really was. There was just so much going on in my head right now that it was hard to really figure out what I was feeling.

I hated to admit it, but I was feeling worse and worse the closer it got to Thursday and the start of the trial. I knew that Daniel must be having similar feelings, that things weren't going to be easy for him either. I also knew that part of my gloom had to do with the depressingly dreary weather outside.

So I was hoping that soup and sandwiches would suit the weather and cheer me up a bit, and that some conversation with my best friend would help me sort out what to do about Daniel's proposition.

"All right, what's going on?" Leanne asked me before I had figured out how to begin.

I grinned ruefully over at her. Of course she would realize that something was wrong. She'd been my best friend since freshman year of high school, and she knew me better than anyone. She could read my moods like a book.

"It's work," I admitted. "And Daniel."

"Uh oh, trouble in paradise?" Leanne asked sympathetically.

I was still worried that telling her about all of this mess would change her view of Daniel yet again. She and my brother, Matt, definitely hadn't been Daniel's number one fan from the start. In fact,

Leanne, who read far more of the tabloids than I did, had cautioned me to stay away from him and never date him at all, even though she'd been on board with me going to work for him from the time we saw the advertisement in the paper.

But when Matt got in an accident and Daniel had proved just how good of a guy he was, driving me to the hospital and bringing us all food, among other things, Leanne and Matt had slowly come around.

I didn't want to undo all of that progress. I wanted Leanne and Matt to like Daniel; he was important to me, and if I had my way, I would keep him in my life for a long time to come. If they didn't support my relationship with him, I just didn't know what I would do.

But I needed her opinion on the question of my taking over temporarily as CEO of McGregor Enterprises. I wasn't expecting her to make the decision for me—nothing like that. But she had always been my sounding board, the person to make me understand my own thoughts and feelings even better than I could on my own.

I couldn't ask her opinion on any of that without telling her why Daniel wouldn't be able to be CEO for the time being. I had to tell her about the trial.

"It's not trouble in paradise, per se," I finally said with a sigh. "But Daniel is going to have to go to court tomorrow."

"Shit, that escalated rather quickly." Leanne said, her eyebrows flying up toward her hair. "What did he do?"

"It's Gerrard—the guy who was Daniel's advisor before me. He's taking Daniel to court for assault, for the night we ran into him at the bar and Daniel punched him." Those were the facts, and I tried to relate them as emotionlessly as possible.

But I could see from the way Leanne's lips tightened that she had strong feelings of her own about the news. "All right," she said evenly. "He'll plead guilty to it, of course. There were photos of the incident. Plus witnesses, plenty of them." Suddenly, she looked even more worried. "He's not asking you to lie as a witness, is he?"

"Of course not!" I said, shocked that she would even suggest that. I thought that she had come around to him, but now, I had to wonder.

Leanne held up both hands. "Sorry, I don't mean to make it sound that way. I'm just trying to get a feel for why you're so upset." She paused. "I mean, I know that you aren't thrilled that he beat this guy up, and I can't blame you for that. But you knew about that already and you still wanted to be with him. So I'm trying to understand what's changed."

"I guess it's not totally about him punching Gerrard. Like you said, I've come to terms with that. But a big trial could really shake things up between the two of us, just when things were getting good. Like, there's no way to keep this out of the press."

"Gerrard won't settle outside of court?" Leanne asked shrewdly.

I shook my head. "Honestly, I didn't even ask Daniel. I assume he already thought of that. He doesn't want to go to trial any more than I want him to." My lips quirked upward briefly. "I actually think he's more frustrated on the amount of time he's going to have to spend in court and not in the office. You know he's a workaholic; he sees this as an affront to the way he lives his whole life."

Leanne grinned and shook her head. "You know, I can see that about him, from everything you've told me," she said. She paused, frowning suddenly. "What is he going to do about that? You said he has to go to trial tomorrow? Have you met whoever his stand-in is going to be? Or is he thinking that it'll be over with quickly enough that you'll be able to cover for him in the interim?"

I grimaced. "Well, yes and no," I said.

"What does that mean?" Leanne asked, looking confused.

"He wants me to take over as CEO while he's tied up in the legal proceedings," I explained.

Leanne whistled under her breath. "Wow," she said. "That's big."

"It is," I agreed grimly.

"You don't sound very happy about it," Leanne said slowly.

"It's not that I'm not happy about it," I said, carefully considering my words. "It's just that I'm not so sure about it. I'm nervous."

"Talk to me," Leanne said simply.

I smiled at her and then took a deep breath. "You know that I want to be CEO someday," I said. "And that's still true. And I do feel that since I've started working for Daniel, I'm closer to that goal. I'm learning valuable knowledge from him, and I do feel like I'm gaining confidence in my ability to make business decisions. He and I are on the same page for a lot of things. And when we're not, either he makes it easy for me to see his point of view or vice versa."

Leanne frowned at me. "So you're just nervous about this?" she asked. "Sounds like you think you could take the job with no problem."

"It's not just nervousness," I said, shaking my head. "Honestly, I just feel like there's so much that I still have to learn. I don't think I'm ready for this—not yet anyway." A wave of unhappiness spread through me as I admitted that to her. I wanted to believe that I was ready for it, that was the thing. After all, hadn't I worked all through school for a position like this? And I had been chomping at the bit for the years since graduation, sure that I deserved something more.

Something just like this. A job that came with a certain amount of responsibility attached. Yet, here it was, and I was shying away from it, sure that I wasn't ready for it yet.

Leanne looked amused. "Daniel doesn't strike me as the kind of guy to try to give you a task he doesn't think you're ready for," she said.

I frowned. "What makes you say that?" I asked.

Leanne shrugged. "Well, from what I've seen of him, he's not only crazy about you, but he also appreciates every one of your strengths. I don't think he's trying to recklessly tear you down, and I also think he cares a great deal about your happiness and your mental state."

I blushed, but I couldn't keep the grin from my face. "Yeah, maybe," I hedged.

Leanne shrugged expansively. "I can't tell you what to do," she said, as though I didn't already realize that. "But I can tell you, I don't think you need to worry so much about this. Maybe you're not 100 percent ready for it yet. But what better learning experience than hands-on trying to run the company? Especially since you haven't been with them forever and you can't just do exactly what you think Daniel would do?"

I shook my head. "If this was some kind of classroom exercise, that would be one thing," I told her. "But as it is, this is a real company. An important one. The decisions I would make as interim CEO could really change people's lives. For the worse, if I'm not careful."

"It has nothing to do with being careful, and you know that," Leanne said, shaking her head. "You've got good instincts. We all know that. Daniel definitely knows that. He's trusting you to make the right decisions on his behalf. That has to mean something, doesn't it?"

"It does." I sighed. "I just don't know if that's enough." I frowned, trying to think of how to explain it to her. But really, what it came down to was that I was scared. I didn't want to mess things up.

"It's only temporary," Leanne reminded me, as though I had spoken out loud. "Whatever you do wrong, Daniel will still be right there to counsel you through it. Or to fix things once his trial is over."

"I don't want to mess things up, though," I said, hating that it sounded like I was whining. But to be honest, hearing how supportive Leanne was of this opportunity, I wondered why I had been so worried in the first place. She had come around to the idea of me dating Daniel, upon my insistence that he was a good guy. Maybe it was time for me to try my hand at being temporary CEO of the company, against my insistence that it might not work out well for anyone.

"I don't know," Leanne said finally. "It just seems to me that this is the perfect chance for you to see what being a CEO is all about, without the real high stakes. Like, if you were going to really become CEO of a company, it wouldn't be with McGregor Enterprises; you've told me that. Because you couldn't just take Daniel's family company away from him for good. So if it were any other company, you'd be walking in there blind. But at least here, you not only know something about the company ahead of time, but you also have Daniel there at your back in the worst-case scenario."

"I guess," I said, starting to see her point of view.

"And besides, if you really screw something up, all you have to do is tell Daniel and he'll find someone else to put in charge in the interim," Leanne added. "What's the worst you can do?"

I cracked a smile at that. "I don't even want to think about it," I told her, but to be honest, her words gave me only relief.

Because the truth was, I really did want to take Daniel up on his offer. For the same reasons that Leanne had said, basically: because this was a low-risk way to really try out being a CEO. And I had never backed down from a challenge before. Daniel's faith in me was flattering, and I trusted him to know what he was talking about.

Not only that, but if I was going to end up in the tabloids either way, I would rather shut them up, give them something other than my relationship with Daniel to talk about. Wouldn't it be nice to read about my business prowess for once, rather than read about what I was wearing out to dinner?

I wasn't so naive as to think that every magazine would print the story with that spin on it. Plenty of them were probably going to write that I was a scheming whore, that I had orchestrated the whole incident with Gerrard, that this was all something we cooked up between us to get money from Daniel.

Maybe that was far-fetched, but I could see it happening.

What I'd like, though, was to see just one article that pointed out that I was making the most of a bad situation, and doing a damned good job of it, too. Maybe that was too much to ask. It would have been easier if I hadn't been there when Daniel first assaulted Gerrard. It would have been easier if we hadn't just come out to the press with our relationship.

But I could dream, anyway.

"Daniel can't possibly expect you to be perfect," Leanne said suddenly. She held up a hand before I could get offended at that. "Come on, we both know that you're not going to do things exactly the way that he would, and he can't expect that of you. What's more, I think from what I've seen, he doesn't expect that of you. He likes that you challenge him, just the same way that you like that working for him challenges you." She was grinning at me, and I had to grin in response.

"If this wasn't what he wanted, would he be offering it to you?" Leanne said firmly. "Enough said."

"There's other things as well," I finally sighed.

"Such as?"

"The media," I said disdainfully.

Leanne shook her head. "I hate to say it, but if you wanted to stay out of the tabloids, you shouldn't have started dating him in the first place. That ship has sailed."

"And you don't think they're going to be even worse about it now that Daniel's on trial for punching a guy who insulted me?" I said wryly.

"There's only so many negative things they can write," Leanne said somewhat dismissively. She paused, drumming her fingers on the tabletop. "Abby, you're smart. You know just what they're going to say about you. Just don't worry about all of that. You've told me before that the guys you do business with don't seem to care. So why let it bother you? Just don't look at it."

"But what about Zach and Layla?" I couldn't help asking.

Leanne smiled at me. "I'm flattered that you're worried about what they would think if they were to read about it," she said. "But Zach is only nine, and Layla is even younger. By the time they're of age to read that kind of crap, it'll be buried underneath the next five hundred scandals." She paused and then shook her head. "Don't you think the media would be harsher on you if they found out you had been offered this position and turned it down?"

"I already thought about that," I admitted. "I just don't know what to do."

Leanne shrugged. "And I can't tell you," she said, stirring her soup for a moment with her spoon. "But what I can tell you is that Daniel was willing to not only sit with you at the hospital for practically the whole weekend when Matt had his accident, but he also came to dinner with us. You've got something good with him, I think what you need to do is figure out how to keep that going."

"Are you saying that my refusing to stand in as interim CEO might ruin our relationship?" I asked, aghast.

Leanne snorted. "No, but if you quit your job at McGregor Enterprises and move to Alaska or somewhere, that just might," she joked. She gave me another serious look. "Abby, I think you'll do an amazing job at this, and if I were you, I'd probably be jumping up and down at the opportunity. But you know I'll support you, whatever you decide. And I'm sure Daniel will as well."

I nodded slowly at her, knowing she was absolutely right. This was an opportunity, no matter how scary it was. It was a chance for me to really prove myself. And I wanted to step up to the challenge, I had to admit. I wanted to prove to myself, as well as to the media, that I wasn't just an attractive woman Daniel had hired.

Maybe that would even help his case with Gerrard, by proving that the former advisor had been slandering me and thus giving Daniel a reason to try to shut him up.

Okay, maybe nothing that extreme, but I could always hope, right?

"Thanks," I said to Leanne.

"You're going to take the job, aren't you?" Leanne asked, grinning at me.

I nodded at her. "I've already taken the job as advisor," I pointed out. "It's not like this will really be all that much different."

Chapter 5

Daniel

I WASN'T SURPRISED when Abby returned from lunch and came directly into my office to see me. She paused in the doorway, though, looking around in surprise. "Damn, boss, it looks like a hurricane went through here," she said.

I sighed, not sure what to say in response to that.

Abby frowned at me, shutting the door carefully behind herself and coming over to my desk, perching precarious on the edge of it. "Is everything okay?" she asked. "You look worried."

I grimaced. "I just have a lot on my plate right now, as you well know," I told her, trying not to react to the close proximity to her. We were rarely this close around the office; we had both decided that the wisest course of action was to maintain a good distance between us at work, to act strictly professional. Indeed, to the casual observer, it probably seemed like we were barely friends outside of the office. We walked into work holding hands, but that was about it.

I just wanted to pull her into my arms, to hold her close, to reassure both her and myself that things were going to be all right. I couldn't do that, though, and I knew it. I took a deep breath and let it out slowly.

"Well, here's one thing off your plate," Abby told me. "I accept the position of interim CEO while you sort things out with Gerrard." She paused, looking around again, and I could see the trepidation in her eyes. "Now, please tell me I don't have to read all of this before tomorrow's meetings!"

I laughed in spite of myself. "Nah, not before tomorrow," I told her. "It's really just here in case you need it. I tried to get together all the information I have about all of our different clients, and the shareholders, and anyone else that you might have to deal with." I paused. "It's a bit tricky because I don't have any idea how long this trial is going to last for."

"That's fair," Abby said, nodding. She chewed at her lower lip. "To be honest, I'm pretty nervous about this whole thing, and all of this isn't making me feel any better." She swept an arm around the room and then shrugged. "I feel like I'm woefully unprepared for this position."

I snorted. "If you really want to know, that's about how I felt when I took the company over from my father," I confessed.

"Bullshit," Abby said, shaking her head. "I bet you'd been going to meetings with him for years by that point. Getting to know the shareholders and the other employees and all of that. Learning to understand how the business operates and its values and everything."

I grimaced and shook my head. "I know you don't believe everything the tabloids say about me, but I have to admit, they were pretty right about me back at the start of things," I told her. "I wasn't always as focused as I am now."

Abby stared at me quizzically for a moment and then nodded slowly. "All right, I'll grant you that," she said. "But at least it was your family's business you were taking over." She made a face. "I just don't want to make some stupid mistake and cost you or the company money. I don't want to screw up."

I stared at her for a moment and then stood abruptly, pulling her into my arms because I just couldn't help it anymore. "Abby, that's ridiculous," I told her.

"No, it isn't," Abby protested, but her arms came around my back as well, her cheek pressing close above my heart. "Mistakes happen."

"Of course they do," I said soothingly. "But I trust you. And I know that mistakes happen. I'm not asking you to be perfect. You don't need to worry about that. I'm not going to be mad at you if you drop the ball on something." I sighed, nuzzling her hair. "I mean, let's be real here, I'm the one who has really dropped the ball. That's exactly why I need you to help me out. If you're willing to."

"I want to," Abby said. "But I'm probably going to have a zillion stupid questions for you to answer. After the first day even."

"And I'll do my best to answer them," I promised her. "Erin's another great resource, believe it or not. She's been with this company for a while now, and she knows things about it that none of the rest of the do, purely because she's the one scheduling all of my meetings and working behind the scenes. She'll be here to help you as well."

"I'd expect you to be more bothered by the idea of giving up your company. Even temporarily," Abby said.

I pulled back to grin down at her. "Is that your way of threatening that I'm never going to get it back?" I asked her.

She looked horrified that I had even suggested that. "No, not at all!" she said. "You'd better come back. It's your family's business, after all."

I sighed and glanced away from her. "I know it is," I said, surprising even myself with the level of bitterness in my tone. "To be honest," I told her carefully, having a hard time getting the words out, "I'm almost excited to have a reason to take a break from it. Not that this is the kind of break I would have chosen for myself."

Abby stared at me as though I had two heads. "I never would have thought I would hear that coming from you," she said, and I could hear a faint tone of bewilderment in her voice.

I winced, realizing how it must sound to her. Given that she thought of me as such a workaholic, she was probably wondering, now, if she even knew me at all. If I'd just been lying to her or putting up a facade all along. If maybe I was exactly the man that the tabloids made me out to be.

"I love this company," I hurried to clarify. "It'll just be nice to step away from the meetings sometimes. I've known for a while now that I need to delegate more. Erin's been hounding me on that one. And honestly, Gerrard was before that." I frowned pensively. "I wonder if that's what got him so frustrated at me." It seemed like such a minor thing, but I supposed it would kind of make sense.

He must have realized that his career with McGregor Enterprises had gone as far as it could, and he had decided to seek out alternatives. I honestly couldn't really blame him for that. At least, not until I considered the way in which he had ultimately sold out.

I shook those thoughts out of my head and bent lower to give Abby a soft kiss on the lips. "I'm going to be around, whatever you need," I promised her. "I just won't be here for meetings and that sort of thing. But it's going to work, and you're still going to see plenty of me."

"Plenty of you?" Abby asked hopefully, her fingers brushing along the bare skin beneath the hem of my shirt.

I laughed and pushed her hands away. "Plenty of me," I promised her, and she grinned up at me, clearly realizing just how flustered that simple touch had gotten me. When this was all over, I was going to show her just how much I really cared about her, I vowed. We'd had one romantic weekend interrupted before, when her brother was in a car accident. Maybe it was time to plan another one.

Not for right now, of course. There was nothing we could do as long as I was tied up in court. But as soon as that was over, we'd see.

"So you're off to court in the morning?" Abby asked quietly.

I nodded at her. "Yeah." I sighed. "I won't have time to swing by the office or anything; I'm supposed to be there pretty early. But like I said, this should be everything that you need, and then you've got Erin. And the rest of the employees as well. But I think you'll do fine."

"How long do you think the trial is going to take?" Abby asked, and I could hear the note of worry in her voice. "And what's going to happen? Do you know what kind of sentence you'll end up with?"

"My lawyer and I have discussed things," I admitted, inclining my head toward her. On the one hand, I didn't want there to be any secrets between the two of us. But on the other hand, I didn't want to worry her unnecessarily. And telling her about all the myriad of punishments I might end up with certainly seemed to be worrying her for no reason. I doubted anything too terrible was going to happen. Sure, it would have been nice to settle outside of court, strictly for privacy reasons. And I was worried about what the jury would think of me.

But at the end of the day, justice would prevail. I was sure of that.

"I have a great lawyer," I finally told Abby. "To be honest, I'm not expecting much to come of this. Gerrard was the one who betrayed me. He sold out my information to the press. I have a good case, a good argument, and at the end of the day, I'm sure we'll come to some agreement. It's more annoying than anything else."

I felt kind of bad telling her that, since there was no way for me to know how things were going to turn out. But on the other hand, if I didn't keep telling myself that things were going to be fine, I was really going to start to panic myself. I couldn't imagine doing jail time. Or even therapy, if those anger management classes were going to keep me away from my business, which they surely would. If nothing else than for the reputation of the business.

But Abby seemed to understand, nodding at me. She leaned against my chest again, her fingers tangled with mine, her thumb stroking over my skin. "I wish you didn't have to deal with this," she said softly. She gave a short laugh. "I honestly wish that we could just get away from all of this madness and drama. Go off somewhere, just the two of us. Really explore our relationship and forget about all of the stress."

My heart ached to hear her say that. Because I knew she deserved much better than this. I reached out to stroke her cheek lightly. "I wish I could take you somewhere now," I told her. "When this is all over, I will."

"Where?" Abby asked, cracking a half-smile.

"Anywhere you want to go," I promised her.

Chapter 6

Abby

I YAWNED AS I SLIPPED into my dress on Thursday morning. I hadn't slept well the night before, tossing and turning, so worried about my new temporary position and all the things that could go wrong. "I didn't keep you up all night, did I?" I asked Daniel, feeling guilty. I should probably have just gone home, but it had been nice to be there with him, to have his silent comfort next to me.

It might not help me sleep, but it did mean a lot to me that he had so much confidence in me.

Daniel glanced over as he buttoned up his shirt and shook his head, making a face. "I had a difficult time sleeping, too," he said, reminding me that he had to be at least as nervous as I was.

I grinned crookedly at him. "We're quite the pair, aren't we?" Daniel snorted. "Would you mind helping me zip up my dress?"

Daniel stepped over behind me, sliding his hands up my bare skin from my waist and then kissing my neck. I groaned, watching our reflection in the full-length mirror.

He looked very handsome in his suit. Strong and important. Smart. Of course, he usually looked good around the office, but today, it was clear that he had taken extra care for his appearance, obviously wanting to project a certain image to the court.

"You look nice," I said, leaning back into him for a moment, drawing strength from his solid warmth.

"Just trying to impress the judge," Daniel responded, winking at me. He pulled away all too soon, but I knew it was for the best. This morning, more than any other morning, we both needed to be on time. I hated the thought of showing up to work without him, though.

We had decided that I would drive myself to work that morning rather than take a cab or private car. Hopefully, any reporters that were there would be expecting me to arrive in Daniel's car at the front of the building as usual. So if I parked in the garage and went up into the building that way, they wouldn't suspect it and I'd be able to slip around them.

I could only hope so. We weren't sure if they had already found out about the trial, but I imagined that some of them must have. Especially since Daniel had explained to me that Gerrard had been leaking information about him to the press for years, getting paid for top-quality information on the CEO's whereabouts. No, this trial probably wasn't a secret, and I wasn't ready to try and answer any questions about anything just yet. Especially not without Daniel there at my side.

Especially not on my first day as CEO. It might only be a temporary change, but it still felt pretty monumental.

Surprisingly, everything went according to plan. I was nervous on the drive in, but I just kept reminding myself to take deep breaths and let them out slowly. It didn't help much, but what could you do?

There were definitely members of the press crowded outside the front of the building, but I barely glimpsed them as I turned left into the parking garage, bringing the car around into Daniel's CEO spot.

CEO. Is this really happening?

I sat in the car for a solid five minutes trying to compose myself. I was sure that the easy smile on my face as I breezed into the office was clearly fake, but again, what could you do?

"Good morning!" Erin chirped when she saw me. "Why don't I give you the rundown for the day?" She led me into Daniel's office and started listing off everything that I should be working on for the day. I was immediately overwhelmed.

Of course, I knew that Daniel did other things than just attend meetings next to me. But I had never quite realized the scope of what he did in his day-to-day work. If the situation hadn't been so serious, I might have laughed about how terrible he was about delegating work. Surely he didn't have to do all of this himself. And it was no wonder that he ended up staying late nearly every evening!

But I knew that without a doubt that wasn't Daniel. He wanted to be firmly involved in his family's business. In every part of it, if he could help it. Still, it made my job pretty difficult now, especially as I looked around the office again, wary of all the stacks of paper he had laid out. Mountains, really. I swallowed hard.

"Hey, you know you're not alone in this," Erin said, clearly reading my dismay.

I looked back over at her in surprise, then remembered what Daniel had said the previous day about her. She had been with this company for a while now, and she knew the ins and outs of it better than almost anyone else.

Sure enough: "Any questions you might have, just let me know," Erin told me. "If I don't know the answer, I may be able to point you in the right direction, either in these files or, if we can't find the answer there—which I doubt since Daniel basically acted like he was preparing for the apocalypse and I can't possibly imagine there being another situation that he didn't prepare notes for—but on the off chance that there is one, I can probably find you someone who can answer the question for you."

"Thank you," I said gratefully. "Seriously, I don't think I could do this without your help."

"Don't worry about it," Erin said, grinning at me. "I'm Daniel's assistant, remember. Now I guess I'm yours temporarily. So whatever you need, you just have to ask." She paused. "And if I do a good enough job, maybe you'll give me a raise, boss?" she joked.

I had to laugh at that. "I don't think I'm ready to start navigating those waters anytime soon," I told her.

"Fair enough," Erin said, winking at me. "So the schedule for today, then. You've got these two conference calls and then that marketing meeting. Then you'll have time for a quick lunch before that sales pitch from some of the company's clients, the ones you were supposed to meet with Daniel."

I nodded. There were a lot of decisions I would need to make today. I didn't even know what the conference calls would be about, although Erin promised me that there were files relating to each one, and I had a little time to brush up on the background information before I sat in on them. And marketing? I didn't know the first thing about marketing, so I really hoped that Daniel didn't expect me to make any decisions on that one.

I was really starting to feel like I was in over my head. I only hoped that Erin couldn't see my panic. Or rather, that no one except Erin would see my panic.

"Have you thought about what you're going to say when they ask you where Daniel is?" Erin asked suddenly. "Because you know, some of them are probably going to want to know."

I blinked at her. How had I not thought about that? I should have asked Daniel what he wanted me to say. I glanced around at all the stacks of papers. "He thought of all of this, but he didn't think of that?" I asked, but the joke fell flat. I sighed. "I suppose I can't tell them that he's sick, because I don't want to lie to them, and they're sure to find out about the trial at some point once the media gets involved."

"Exactly," Erin said, nodding at me. "I'd suggest something like, 'He had other personal matters to attend to', just something vague but truthful. And tell them that if they'd like more information, they're going to have to talk to Daniel directly."

I nodded. That made sense. I tried to get those words stuck in my head so they'd be ready the first time I had to answer the question.

Erin smiled sympathetically at me. “Hang in there,” she said. “And you know where to find me.”

With that, she headed out of the office, leaving me in there all alone. I couldn’t help feeling, as I sat in Daniel’s chair behind his broad desk, that I was an imposter, like a little kid pretending to go to work as his parents.

But I was trained for this, I reminded myself. And Daniel thought that I could do it. His faith in me gave me confidence—it made me stronger.

I took another deep breath and picked up the brief on that morning’s conference call. I could do this. In any case, it was too late to change my mind now. In for a penny in for a pound, as my dad used to say.

Chapter 7

Daniel

I WALKED OUT OF THE courtroom after the first day feeling grim. My lawyer clapped me on the shoulder, saying something about how things were going to go better tomorrow, but I barely heard him. I rolled my shoulders to attempt to release the tension and prepared to walk outside, knowing for sure that there would be members of the press waiting to pester me with questions as I worked my way to the car. Another day.

I glanced down at my phone and was surprised to see I had a message from Abby. She had sent it after lunch, so I hadn't had a chance to see it. I felt a moment of panic, hoping that nothing had gone horribly wrong on her first day at work. But I smiled faintly when I saw the message, which had been sent not too long ago: *Hurry home, dinner's almost ready!*

After a day like this, there was nothing I wanted more than to go home to Abby and a good, home-cooked meal.

For a moment, I wondered whether she meant my place or hers. After all, the "home" part was pretty vague. But then again, she had been spending most nights at my place lately. It was a pretty safe bet that she meant my place. She had a key, after all. And either way, I wanted to get out of my suit and into something more comfortable. Might as well head home, see if she was there, and if not, then head over to her place.

When I got to my place, though, the heavenly aroma of warm food wafted through the house from the moment I stepped in the front door. I almost groaned with relief as I kicked off my shoes and padded into the kitchen, shedding my suit jacket over the back of a chair and making a beeline for Abby, who was over by the stove.

"Hey," I said, wrapping my arms around her and burying my face against the side of her neck.

"Hey, yourself," she said, a smile in her voice as she leaned back against me for a moment.

"It smells amazing," I said.

"Chicken pot pies," Abby told me. "Leanne gave me the recipe. Apparently they're one of Matt's new favorite fall foods, and it sounded like just the perfect thing for the weather."

"Definitely sounds good," I sighed. I pulled away from her with regret.

"How was your first day?" she asked, turning to face me.

I shook my head. "It didn't go very well," I admitted. "There were plenty of witnesses from that night at the bar, and their recollection of the evening definitely favors Gerrard." I paused and shook my head. "I'm actually surprised they were able to round up so many of them."

"Yikes," Abby said, looking worried. She paused. "I know you said your lawyer has a strong case, but are you sure that you don't need me to testify on your behalf? I'm the reason that you got in the fight in the first place. And I was the only one who was really listening, probably, before the fight broke out. Maybe I could paint a more accurate picture for the judge and jury."

She sounded so earnest, and I could tell that she really wanted to help. But I couldn't ask her to do that. I knew what her feelings were on that night, and I knew that, like she had said, I deserved to face the consequences for my actions. Besides, I knew she didn't approve of that fight. I didn't want her to have to relive it.

And the media. They would be all over it. I had promised that I would do whatever was in my power to keep her safe from those wolves. Throwing her right into the midst of this trial would be the opposite of that.

I leaned in to kiss her gently but shook my head as I pulled away. "Don't worry about it," I told her. "I'm sure the lawyer has everything in hand, and I don't want to drag you into all of it. But I do appreciate the offer."

Abby looked like she wanted to protest, but eventually, she nodded, albeit unhappily. I was spared having to respond to that look by the oven timer going off. Abby turned to pull the pot pies out of the oven.

"Those look perfect." I groaned, already salivating just at the look of them. Abby grinned over her shoulder at me, and that was that.

We sat down to a peaceful dinner together, with Abby catching me up on what had happened at the office that day in my absence. I smiled hearing how perfectly she had handled a disagreement in the marketing team meeting. She looked uncertain, though, like she wasn't sure she had made the right decision. I assured her that she had and was rewarded with another bright smile.

With each new smile from her, I felt more of my stress from the day melt away, until I could finally just breathe again. Abby favored me with one last smile as she grabbed my empty plate, then brought it over to the sink.

"Let's just leave the dishes for tonight," I told her, following her and putting my hands on her hips, pressing up against her. I brushed some of her hair back, kissing her neck, and I could feel her shudder against me. It sent lust zinging straight for my cock, which was already somewhat interested after having listened to her detail her competent work as a CEO that day.

I never would have thought it would be such a turn-on to find a woman who was so brilliant at running my family business.

Abby turned toward me, putting her hands on my shoulders to steady herself. "Whatever you say, boss," she breathed.

I captured her lips in a heated kiss, pushing her back against the countertop, unable to resist the urge to slide a leg between hers and grind against her. She moaned into the kiss, her fingers creeping around the back of my neck to pull me closer, until the kiss was almost bruising in its fiery intensity.

When I let go of her, she looked raw and open already, as though we were already fucking rather than simply making out in the kitchen. I kept my dark, smoldering gaze on her as I grabbed her hands and walked backward toward my bedroom.

It took us a while to make it there. I couldn't quit kissing her, pressing her up against the wall in the hallway, the banister, any surface we came across. As I kissed her, my fingers worked at the zipper on the back of her dress, slowly dragging it down, tracing her spine with featherlight touches. She was giggling by the time we made it to the top of the stairs, but her laughter died on a needy whimper as I slid the dress off her shoulders, carelessly letting it fall to the floor, before I pulled her nearly-naked body against mine again, fingers finding the cleft between her thighs.

Chapter 8

Abby

I WAS PRACTICALLY SHAKING with need by the time Daniel led me into his bedroom and started stripping off his own clothes. I fell back on the bed, somehow already nearly naked, and watched him with a hooded gaze, absently trailing my fingers across my own skin to satiate the desperate desire coursing through my body.

I honestly didn't know how I was this turned on. But somewhere between the kitchen and his bedroom, my lust had become almost overpowering. Part of it had to do with the approving looks Daniel had been giving me during dinner as I told him about my first day as his stand-in at the office. There was something about knowing that he really did believe I could do the job.

It also had to do with the fact that, I was sure, we both needed to blow off a little steam after a stressful day. It was nice to lean into his body, to find a place where I fit so well, to turn my face up toward his and forget all about my worries.

But there was something more to this than just blowing off steam. Daniel was more gentle with me than he had ever been, running his hands down my sides, trailing soft touches around the edges of my nipples. When he finally pushed his fingers into me, he set a slow, easy rhythm, focusing more on varying the pressure against my walls than on quick thrusts.

He held me close to him as he plunged his member deep into my core, covering territory that his fingers hadn't been able to reach. I gasped, clinging to him, moving my body with his.

It didn't take much for him to bring me over the edge—just a few correctly placed thrusts and I was cumming, his name on my lips. But he continued to rock into me, chasing pleasure of his own, and my core continued to burn with rapidly increasing need as I whimpered and begged for more.

I could tell that he was close as well, his muscles drawing taut through his chest and abs, his face twisting in surprise as lust spiked sharply through his body. He pulled me into one final, searing, all-encompassing kiss, his tongue desperately seeking mine as his hips stuttered off rhythm. He was all around me, inside me, filling me and keeping me safe.

I spilled again, unable to help it, my walls clenching around his twitching, spurting cock. My body sank into the memory-foam mattress, and a deep exhaustion settled over me, a combination of the sex, the crazy day, and my terrible sleep from the night before. Although I still didn't feel any more confident in my position as McGregor Enterprises' CEO, I knew then that I wouldn't have any trouble sleeping that night.

A slow smile spread across my face as Daniel maneuvered us so that my head was resting on his chest. He bent to kiss my forehead. I could hear his heartbeat still thudding from exertion, a reminder of what we had just done, as though the loose and limber feeling of my body wasn't proof enough.

Again, those three words. *I love you,* I thought. But I was too exhausted to give voice to them now, and anyway, Daniel no doubt knew that without my saying it.

I relaxed against him, enjoying the way he toyed with my hair as I fell asleep curled around him.

Chapter 9

Daniel

FRIDAY WAS THE FIRST day I heard my lawyer sound anything less than confident about this trial. As Jude and I prepped that morning before entering the courtroom, she suddenly said, "You know, things could get dicey with this trial."

I grimaced at how serious she looked, at least thanking my lucky stars that I had a whole legal team in my court. She was my lawyer's co-council and just as determined to fix this... "You already told me about the possible sentences," I reminded her.

"I know," Jude said, nodding. "I just want to make sure you're prepared. I'll do everything I can to get the jury on your side, but the public is really getting involved with this case. It's all over social media, and to be honest, the facts aren't exactly on our side. All the chaos is working to Gerrard's advantage."

"I know." I sighed. I had avoided looking at any of the news that morning, but Austin had sent me a message letting me know that there was a lot of bad press out there. Honestly, though, I wasn't so much worried for myself than I was about how all of this would affect McGregor Enterprises and, by proxy, Abby. I didn't want to think about how hard it could make her position as interim CEO, even though obviously none of this mess was her fault.

I shrugged at Jude. "There's nothing we can do except plead our case, right?"

"Right," she said.

We headed into the courtroom not long thereafter. Gerrard's lawyer basically annihilated my case, reminding the jury again and again that it wasn't just about my beating up my former employee, but I had also fired him for "uncertain reasons," hinting at what those reasons might have been, in light of who I'd been at the bar with that night. They talked about how long Gerrard had been at McGregor Enterprises, and all the long hours that he'd "had" to pull with me.

I was fuming. Half of what they said was only partially true, and the other half, well. The way that they were embellishing things was clearly biasing the jury.

When I took the stand, I was determined to clear things up, to tell the jury the whole truth of the matter. But with the questions I was asked, especially during cross-examination, it only became more and more apparent to me that the jury was clearly on Gerrard's side. I could see them nodding away, scribbling notes, frowning with their arms crossed over their chests as I tried to defend my actions.

I wanted to tell them all about how Gerrard had been selling information about me for a couple years, about how he was in violation of his contract, about how he clearly had some sort of vendetta against me. But after talking to Jude about it, I knew that I couldn't bring all of that up. If I wanted to countersue Gerrard, then I needed to do that the legal way. I couldn't just introduce that information into this trial.

And on top of that, there was still that lack of evidence. It would just be hearsay if I started going off about it in the middle of the trial, and I was worried how Gerrard's lawyer might try to spin that. It wasn't like we could introduce members of the press as witnesses, even if I could get one or two of them to agree to testify against Gerrard.

There was no way for the jury to really understand the reasons behind my punching Gerrard.

No, it was very clear: I had lost the case. I just had to wonder what the sentencing would be.

Jude didn't think the judge was going to be too harsh. It was my first offense, after all, and I did a lot of charity work thanks to my business. The maximum sentence for assault in Chicago was a year in jail and/or fines of up to $2500, but Jude was pretty sure I wouldn't have to serve any jail time. Especially not if I agreed to go to anger management classes for a month or so in light of the trial. I hated that that would be another waste of my time, another thing drawing me away from work and Abby, but then again, so would time in jail.

But I was starting to get a little worried, based on the way that the jury was looking at me. It wasn't about the money. Damn, I would pay him ten times as much as the maximum fine, plus lawyer fees and whatever the fuck else. If he just hadn't had to bring this to *court*. It was too late for that now, though.

At the end of the day, after a quick recess, the judge was back with the verdict: a fine of $2500, plus all of Gerrard's legal fees. No jail time, but anger management classes and some community service. It was a pretty light sentencing, all things told.

But it still stuck in my craw. Especially as I had to walk out of there, with flashbulbs going off left, right, and center, the press peppering me with questions about the trial, about my new advisor, about whether Abby really stood beside me through all of this.

Worse was the text from Austin about the morning's gossip columns. Apparently, they'd caught Abby on her way into work that morning and she'd grimaced her way through a few questions before security managed to get her into the building safely. My fingers clenched into fists, and I wished I could go back to that night at the bar and punch Gerrard all over again, just for doing this.

I should have been there for Abby. I should have walked into that building with her, kept her safe from the press. None of this should ever have happened. We should have been able to stick to our nice morning routine we'd established, walking hand and hand into work and coming home together at the end of every day.

No, the money didn't matter. I'd pay Gerrard whatever it took. I was just pissed because that asshole had won. But at least it was all over now, quickly, and I didn't need to waste any more time on him. Hopefully, this was the last that I would ever see of him.

I got in my car and headed home, eager to see Abby and find out how her day was.

Chapter 10

Abby

IF I THOUGHT I WAS nervous going into work on Thursday morning, it was nothing compared to how I felt on Friday evening, waiting for Daniel to come home. The whole day had been a shitshow for me, but I had also seen online that he lost against Gerrard. Amazing, honestly, that the stories were already up when the trial had pretty much just concluded. But I was grateful to them so that I would know in advance of the mood that Daniel would be in when he got home.

I could tell from his expression in the photos alongside the news stories that he was pissed with the way the trial had turned out. What I wanted was to make him forget about all of that, to have something like a repeat of the previous night: cook a good meal for the two of us, go upstairs with him afterward, fall into bed together. This morning, waking up had been such a pleasure. Daniel had still been there in bed next to me, his hands warm against my skin as he held me close.

It had been the perfect morning, really. Until I had gotten to the office.

I sighed and ran a hand back through my hair. After my first day at the office hadn't been so bad, I honestly had let my guard down today. And that was stupid of me. I knew that. Now, I was waiting for Daniel to come home, and all I could think about was the bad news I had to tell him on top of everything else he had already been through that day.

I had practically paced a hole in the floor by the time Daniel got home. He paused in the doorway of the living room, frowning at me. I saw a flicker of concern in his eyes, despite the tight pinch of anger in his expression. "What's wrong?" he asked.

"I made a mistake at work today," I admitted. "Just like I knew I would." I couldn't help how miserable I sounded about it. I still felt stupid just thinking about it.

Daniel's anger flashed into real fury on his face for a moment, and I almost flinched back. I probably would have if we hadn't had half the room between us still. I knew, instinctively, that Daniel would never hurt me. But in that moment, he sure seemed pissed.

"I saw the articles," he said. "You got cornered on your way into the building." He shook his head sharply. "I should have been there. Or I should have found someone to be there for you. Hired a private security guard or something. I never should have put you in that situation. But seriously, don't worry about it. It was nice to read that you still profess to support me, even though, what was it that they said? I've shown time and again that I'm 'only capable of acting on my impulses and not planning anything long-term for the future'?"

The bitterness in his voice threw me for a moment. I had speculated before that the news articles about him must bother Daniel more than he let on, but I had never heard him talk about them like this before. I took a hesitant step toward him, forgetting for the moment that I had more bad news to deliver, because that press junket hadn't been what I wanted to talk about at all. In fact, I had nearly forgotten about that incident in light of everything else that had happened that day.

Daniel's face softened, and he gave me a tight smile. "Sorry," he said in a quiet voice. "What I'm trying to say is that I'll try not to let anything like that happen ever again." His face twisted again, this time with unhappiness more than anger. "The good news is that the trial's over. Gerrard won. I'm not happy about the outcome, but at least I don't have to do any jail time." He shook his head. "I just still can't believe he won. But the point is, I'll be back to work with you on Monday morning, so you won't have to face the press alone again."

"I appreciate that," I said slowly. But I had to wonder whether he was really going to let me come back to work as usual on Monday when he heard about the other part of the day. "But I actually made another mistake." I took a deep breath, barely able to meet Daniel's eyes. "You know I had that meeting this afternoon, with Duncan Flannigan?"

"Yes," Daniel said, sounding wary.

"The meeting went really well, but afterward, instead of walking him out, I had to rush right into the next meeting. Duncan and I went a little bit overtime, I guess, and I was already a couple minutes late for that next meeting. And it's not like he hasn't been to the office before, so I figured he knew the way out."

Daniel's eyebrows knit together. "What are you trying to tell me—that he somehow managed to get lost in our office building?" he asked.

"Well, no," I said slowly. "But when I came out of the next meeting, he was still there, hanging around and chatting with some of the other employees."

Daniel looked confused, and I couldn't blame him. I had been shocked when I realized what they were chatting about as well. Because at first, I had just stupidly assumed that somehow Duncan Flannigan and Judy Mannheim were friends. After all, Judy had worked for McGregor Enterprises for a while and Duncan had been a client for a long time as well.

But then Erin had come up to me, eyes wide. "He's been snooping around the office trying to find out information about Daniel," she had told me.

"What kind of information?" I had asked.

"Well, he asked me if I had ever slept with him," she had admitted.

Daniel frowned. "Who was he chatting with?" he finally asked.

"Apparently, he went around to all the women in the office and asked personal questions about you, including if any of them had ever had...sexual relations with you."

It was so quiet in that mansion that you could have heard a pin drop. I dared a look up at Daniel's face, and I wasn't sure that I had ever seen him that angry before, not even the night that he had punched Gerrard.

"I kicked him out as soon as I realized what he was doing," I hurried to say. But I knew that that didn't change what had happened. I still felt sick with guilt about it. Because it wasn't just about the information that he might have collected, and I didn't even know what all he might have learned. But it was more that he had the audacity to ask those questions at all.

Daniel had put me in charge of the office. He had trusted me to keep order in the office, and I hadn't. And I knew just how much Daniel cared about all of his employees. I knew that he wouldn't be happy about this situation. Even if nothing got out to the press, he had still made everyone in the office uncomfortable.

And it was all my fault. There were any number of things I could have done differently. I could have walked him out of the office like I normally would have. I couldn't believe I had attempted to extend the contract we had with him. I should have been able to see through him, to see what kind of guy he really was. Not the kind of guy that we wanted to do business with, that was for sure.

But I hadn't seen any of the signs, and now, looking up at Daniel, I couldn't help feeling like I had failed him.

Chapter 11

Daniel

I STARED AT ABBY IN shock. What the hell had she just said? Duncan Flannigan, walking around the office asking all the female employees if any of them had ever slept with me? I had worked with Duncan for years now; he was one of our most loyal clients. I couldn't believe it.

I shook my head. "Look, I don't know what you think you overheard—" I began.

Abby's head snapped up, and I saw a flash of anger in her eyes to match the frustration in my own. "What I thought I overheard?" she asked incredulously. "I'm not just telling you shit that I overheard."

"So, what, Duncan asked you about your relationship with me?" I asked her disparagingly. It wasn't really that I was mad at her. I was just pissed at the whole situation. First Gerrard, now Duncan. Two men I had worked with forever, two men I had trusted. It seemed like nothing was sacred anymore, though.

I might not have lost much in the trial today, but I had lost more than enough for me to feel like I needed to start rethinking my personal allegiances. But who could I trust?

Abby. I could trust Abby. But even as I took a step toward her, she was shaking her head and stepping back. "Oh no," she said. "You don't just get to say shit like that and then pretend like there's nothing wrong," she snapped.

I winced. "I know," I agreed. "And I'm sorry. It's just been a long day, and I'm a little confused. Did Duncan talk to you or not?"

"He didn't talk to me," Abby said icily. "But Erin says he asked her about her sexual relations with you, and she says that he talked to nearly every woman in the office about the same thing. So, sure, maybe it's hearsay. But I trust Erin. Don't you?"

"Of course I trust Erin," I said, fighting the urge to groan. "Abby, look, I'm sorry. I didn't mean to say it like that. All I'm saying is that I just want to understand what happened a little better. You can give me that, can't you?"

"You're the boss, boss," Abby said snidely. This time, it was no longer a joke shared between the two of us. No, this time, she said it like if I wasn't her boss, she would be walking away right now.

What a misunderstanding. All I wanted to tell her was how glad I was to be home, to see her, to be done with this stupid trial. It might not have gone the way that I wanted things to go, but it wasn't like I really needed the money. All I could think of on the way home was how lucky I was that at the end of the day, I still had Abby in my life. That was what I really cared about right now.

But then with this whole thing at work, whatever she was trying to tell me, it felt like I was just purposefully pushing her away almost. Abby looked like she might cry, even, and all I wanted was to step closer to her, to take her into my arms and apologize. But the way she stepped away from me made it clear that she wanted nothing to do with me right now.

"Abby, what happened?" I asked, hearing the desperation in my voice as I did so.

"Duncan went around the office asking all the available women if they had ever had relations with you. I caught him near the end of his rounds and threw him out of the office." Here, she looked even more uncertain. "And I told him that we would never do business with him again."

"Good," I growled. Duncan might be one of our oldest, most reliable clients, but if what Abby had said was true, and I felt certain that it was or else she wouldn't have said that, then I had no desire to ever do any business with the other man again.

One by one, it seemed like I was cutting all of the older guys out of our business deals, from Gerrard to Duncan. But there was nothing else I could do.

Was this the way that the business world was supposed to be? Somehow, I had never pictured things being this way, back when I was first in charge of the business. I had naively thought that somehow, things would get better and better, year after year. That at the end of the day, I would create some core group of people I worked with all the time, who knew me and the business, guys who shared the same values as me.

That couldn't be further from the truth. I was starting to learn that naivety and ideals had nothing to do with the real business world.

I shook my head, pressing my fingertips against my eyeballs. "So what else happened?" I finally asked Abby.

"What do you mean?" she asked.

I stared blankly at her for a moment. "I just assumed there was more to it," I told her. "You told me that something had gone wrong. That you'd made a mistake."

"I fired one of our best clients," Abby reminded me.

I immediately shook my head. "Abby, I would have done exactly the same thing," I told her. "If I had been running late for a meeting, I wouldn't have seen Duncan out. Same as you, I would have assumed that he would just leave, like normal. Asking prying questions like that to my employees, I never could have suspected it. And if I had caught him doing that, then I would have terminated our contracts with him."

Abby stared at me for a long moment, and I could see that she was seeking reassurance in my face. Again, I wanted nothing more than to hold her. But again, she stepped back away from me, her gaze turning away to the side. "I think I should just head home for the night," she said dully.

"Abby, no," I said, reaching for her. "I want you here."

Abby shook her head, though. "I have a lot of things I need to think over," she said.

"Like what?" I asked, actually puzzled. "Maybe I can help. Be your sounding board, if you will."

"I don't think so," Abby told me, and it was like a knife to the heart. I flinched back, but I didn't know what to say to her. She sighed. "I just don't want to talk right now. I can tell that you're pissed about the trial and all of the work stuff. And I just feel frustrated and out of sorts. Let's give it a night or two. We'll figure it out later. I'm going to go home."

As she turned to head for the door, I wished that I could think of something to say to her, something to make her stop, to come back, to talk things out with me. I wanted to convince her that I wasn't upset, that I wanted to talk things over with her. That I was happy to come home to her, that I wanted to just curl up on the couch with her tonight, maybe put on a shitty movie, cuddle, and relax.

I wanted a place that felt like home. That was all I had ever wanted. And with her, this place could almost feel like home.

But there she went, striding in quick steps away from me, carefully closing the door behind her. I stared at the solid wood, the echoes of the shutting door still resonating in my ears.

Had I lost her again? What had even happened just now? How did I make things better? I knew I couldn't possibly figure out how to make things better without first figuring out just what it was I had screwed up in the first place. And I was afraid that to figure that out, I would have to go back to that night at the bar with Gerrard.

The money might not matter to me. But that didn't mean there were no punishments and that I hadn't screwed up. No, Abby had cooled things off with me once because she didn't want anything to do with the kind of guy who beat up his former trusted advisor in a bar. Now, no doubt, she was thinking about all the other terrible things about me, things that the media had printed over the years.

Only half of those things were true, of course, but she couldn't know which things were true and which were false. And at the end of the day, I supposed it didn't really matter. At the end of the day, I just wasn't a good enough guy. I could never hope to deserve someone like Abby.

I headed into the office, my gut churning with guilt and loneliness. With careful, measured movements, I poured a couple fingers of whiskey into a glass. Then, I sat down with my view over the city of Chicago, alone again in the night.

How many of those lights out there hid people who were just as lonely as me?

None of them, I was sure. There was no way there was anyone in the world who was as lonesome as I was at that precise moment.

Chapter 12

Abby

I HONESTLY COULDN'T tell you why I stormed out of Daniel's on Friday night. I had been so relieved when he finally told me that he would have handled the Duncan situation in exactly the same way as I had. That he would have terminated the contract with Duncan as well. Because that was what I had really been worried about, that he wouldn't understand what I had done. That he would tell me I didn't have the authority to do something like that, or I had cost the business a vital account. I had expected that he would fire me.

But in the end, he seemed to understand and to support my decision. It was everything I had ever wanted to hear from him. But at the end of the day, I couldn't help thinking about the rest of it.

He hadn't taken my story at face value, not at first. He had all but accused me of lying to him, or stretching the truth at the very least. He had sounded so angry at *me*, somehow, when he had asked me if Duncan had asked me anything about my relationship with him. Almost as though Daniel was just angry about our relationship in general. Almost as though he didn't want me there.

And maybe he didn't. I had been there so often, almost every night lately. Maybe Daniel needed his space. Maybe I should have realized that when he was pissed off, as he was bound to be after the trial, that he wouldn't want me around. I was stupid for putting myself in that situation. I had to go home. I had to let him know he wasn't stuck with me every day, not if he didn't want that.

I just wished I had realized it sooner, before I had overstayed my welcome.

Now, Saturday morning, I was alone in my apartment. It had been a while since I'd even been here, and I had to admit, waking up on my own wasn't anything that I really wanted. No, it was much nicer to fall asleep stretched out beside Daniel, to wake up in the morning with his arms curled around my body, my head pillowed on his firm torso.

Instead, Saturday morning brought empty, cold sheets and an ache in my gut that nothing would fill. I wanted to go over to Daniel's, to tell him I was sorry, that I would be more independent from now on, that he didn't have to feel guilty about kicking me out from time to time.

But then again, that probably wasn't what he wanted to hear. "Kicking me out" implied that I would overstay my welcome again. And guilty? I was the one who should be feeling guilty. I was the one who was single-handedly ruining our relationship, both at work and here at home.

The good thing about the fact that I hadn't been home in a while was that everything could use a bit of a light clean. I attacked the place, dusting in spots that hadn't seen the light of day since probably before I had moved in. But I didn't feel any better by the time I was done.

It didn't help that Daniel called halfway through my cleaning spree. I debated picking up the call. But the more I thought about it, the more that seemed like a bad idea. I still felt like there were things I needed to sort through from the night before, and I wasn't going to do that if I just went rushing back to him. Besides, I didn't want him to think that I was too needy.

He had gotten angry with me. That was the main sticking point to all of it. Beyond the neediness and the guilt, there was the fact that he had been angry at *me*. I hadn't expected that. I had never expected that. And I still would never expect Daniel to hit me or otherwise physically hurt me. But at the same time, the physical wasn't everything in a relationship.

Could I be with someone who got angry like that? Could my emotions handle it? I wasn't so sure. I hadn't been sure before, when Daniel punched Gerrard, and now, I felt even less sure, having seen that anger directed toward me, albeit in a muted form.

I scrubbed out the inside of the fridge, trying to pretend that the tears in the corner of my eyes were from the smell of the cleaning agent.

I just couldn't help feeling foolish. It seemed like somehow, I had pegged Daniel totally wrong. Like I had misunderstood our relationship and what I was to him. Like I had tried to make him into a good guy, the kind of guy he had never been to begin with.

The more the afternoon dragged on, the more certain I made myself that something had been wrong from the start. Daniel had never really been the guy I had thought he was. He had never been the guy I had somehow convinced Matt and Leanne that he was. No, he was just what all the tabloids said he was: angry and rude and given to rash impulses. That was it.

Dating me was probably just an impulse thing. He couldn't keep his hands off me. I couldn't expect anything more, when the same was basically just as true for me. It was just an impulse for me to like Daniel like this.

But of course, these were impulses I never should have acted on. There was the difficulty.

Around 3:00 p.m., I got on my computer and started looking up articles about him. Who was this guy I had been dating? If anything, I knew that the articles about the trial were bound to give me clues.

After scrolling through a dozen of the articles, I felt sick to my stomach. Sure enough, Daniel's name was everywhere. There were hundreds of articles out about the assault charges already, some sticking to the bare facts of the trial and others embellishing their articles with anecdotes about other incidents in Daniel's past. Another altercation at another bar. Rumors about loud verbal fights in office meetings.

And everywhere, pictures of him. Angry pictures of him.

The worst article by far, though, was the one with the headline: *Does Abby James Really Know the Man Behind the Smile?*

I swallowed hard, staring at that headline. Did I know the man behind the smile?

The truth was that no matter how many doubts I had about him, I just couldn't believe I could have been so wrong about him. Hell, I had never had such a problem judging people in the business world. There was no way I could have so misjudged Daniel. If I had even suspected he was capable of anger like these stories said, I would never have let him anywhere near Zach and Layla.

Or myself, really. I had to hope that I could see past the smile and the good looks and know who this man was. I had to hope that this time, I knew how to protect myself. That by now, I knew what kind of threats I needed to protect myself from.

I sighed, putting down my phone and rubbing at my eyes. I wanted to call Daniel back, but I felt more confused now than I had the night before. It wouldn't be fair to show up at Daniel's place to tell him all my fears that maybe I had messed up and ended up with the wrong guy all over again. That wouldn't be fair to him.

Not least of which because I was sure he was still recovering from the trial and the aftermath, angry with the circumstances and not good company for anyone. I should give him some time to calm down and center himself first. I was certain that was the best course of action.

I thought back to that stupid headline. Was I so sure of it? Was I sure that I knew the "man behind the smile"?

The damn media. I couldn't believe I was even thinking things like that. But having Daniel yell at me had really unsettled something inside of me. I couldn't think of him as a terrible man, not even close. But he wasn't the saint I had made him out to be in the rose-colored glasses that I seemed to constantly wear around him.

My phone rang again, and my heart leapt, hoping beyond hope that it was Daniel calling me back again. This time, I would answer it. I didn't know what I would say to him, but I knew that we needed to chat in person. I needed to hear his side of things. I needed to know what kind of a past this man really had.

I thought I deserved that. I was pretty sure of it, anyway.

But it wasn't Daniel calling me after all. Instead, it was Leanne. I sighed and took a deep breath, but I knew that this was one call that I couldn't avoid. Leanne would be too worried if I didn't answer the call, if not now then at some point today. She'd have read all the coverage on the trial, and she would want to know how we were holding up.

We, because she would no doubt expect me to be there by Daniel's side.

For a moment, there was something in me that ached to decline the call with Leanne, all so that I could get on the phone with Daniel instead. To tell him I was sorry for the previous night, for the way the trial had gone, for the way I had handled things with Duncan, for the way I had told him I had handled things with Duncan.

Not that any of those apologies would solve anything if he just wanted some space.

Not that I was sure that I wanted to apologize and go see him right now when I knew he could still be so angry. Or possibly even angrier than he had been the last time I had seen him.

In that moment, I realized the crux of it, what it really came down to: I was scared of Daniel. And I hated that feeling. What was more, he didn't deserve for me to feel that way. He had never done anything to hurt me before, and I didn't believe that he would. My fears were ungrounded. But logic couldn't change the way I felt in my heart.

I couldn't call Daniel right then. Better to get the call with Leanne over with, though, before she thought of all the difficult questions to ask. "Hey," I said weakly when I picked up the phone.

"Hey!" Leanne said, and I could tell from the false cheer in her voice that she could hear the unhappiness in my one-word answer. "This news is all so terrible. I just wanted to call and make sure that you were okay and to see if you needed anything. I'm so sorry for how things happened at the trial."

I sighed, trying to think of what to say to that. Should I tell her about the night before? Should I tell her about Duncan? But no. Despite Daniel's assurances that he would have treated the Duncan situation the same way, I still felt foolish about it all. I never should have misjudged the man like that. And not only that, but once I found out that I had misjudged him, I should have elevated the issue to Daniel. I didn't even really have the ability to fire people; I was just Daniel's advisor.

I had overstepped. Daniel really had every right to yell at me.

But he hadn't even yelled at me over that, I reminded myself. No, he had yelled at me because he didn't even believe me when I told him about Duncan. Because he didn't trust my instincts, let alone trust my ability to run an office. And why should he? After all, I was just a pair of legs he had hired.

I couldn't let Gerrard's words get to me, though. Surely Erin or someone else would have taken pity on me, or at least been jealous and spiteful toward me, if Daniel had really slept with all the available women in the office before moving on to me?

"Hey, you okay over there?" Leanne asked, drawing me back to the present conversation.

"Yeah, everything's fine," I said faintly. I cleared my throat. "Things aren't quite as bad as what the media would have you believe," I added wryly, wishing I could believe those words in that statement.

The rest of the conversation with Leanne was a blur, mainly me telling her that we didn't need any help. She seemed certain that there must be a ring of media outside of Daniel's mansion, and maybe there was. I wouldn't know since I wasn't there. All I could do was tell her that we were fine, that we didn't need anything. I knew that part of her desire to help out came in response to how helpful Daniel had been when Matt was in the hospital.

That was barely any time at all ago. How had things gone so wrong so quickly?

Finally, I managed to get off the phone with Leanne. Not that there was much else that I needed to do that afternoon. My desire to call Daniel had waned; it was probably for the best that I give him a little more time to cool off.

And best to give myself a little more time to get over what it was I had done. To get things straight in my head, to come to terms with it. To figure out if I could ever be a CEO one day, or what I was going to do if not. Would I be happy just being an advisor for the rest of my life? Never having any real control, but also not having to worry about the responsibilities?

I hated that I was even questioning that. And after only two days of being a temporary CEO as well. I knew, now, that I should have pushed back harder when Daniel had suggested having me as his stand-in during the trial. I should have told him that I didn't feel ready for it, that I didn't feel prepared.

But instead, I had let him put me in a bad situation, one that I had been uncomfortable in. I had no one to blame except myself.

I sighed when my phone buzzed with a text from him. *You have every reason to ignore me. I'm sorry for how I behaved. When you're ready, can we talk about it?*

I could practically hear the guilt and pain in his voice. At least he clearly knew that his yelling had been out of line. But that didn't make me feel any better about the whole situation. No, I had to figure some things out in my head before I was ready to talk to him about any of it. I just had to hope he would understand.

If not, maybe it would just be proof that he was just the man I had tried to convince myself that he wasn't.

I sighed. Why did loving him have to be so difficult sometimes?

Chapter 13

Daniel

I SHOULD HAVE KNOWN that I wasn't going to be able to avoid the world forever. When Abby had walked out of my place on Friday night, I had been hurt and confused and, most of all, alone. I had drunk myself into a stupor and ended up passing out in an armchair in my study for a while, until the diffuse light of dawn was just brushing the world outside. I had woken with a terrible crick in my neck, feeling no better about things than I had the night before.

In fact, I felt worse. Now, in the light of day, I realized just how badly I had fucked up. I had yelled at Abby. I still remembered the way she had stepped back away from me. Like she wanted nothing to do with me.

And why should she? I had known how worried she was about the idea of being my interim CEO. I never should have pushed her. Because I had pushed her, for all my talk of letting her make her own decision. I had never made it clear to her that there was really any other option. I had pushed her into a role she didn't feel comfortable with, she'd had to make a difficult decision, and she had walked away from the whole thing with her confidence shattered.

Then, instead of building her back up again, I had torn her even further down. I had acted like she couldn't possibly know what was going on around the office, like she was acting irrationally.

The truth was, I had just been so shocked by the very idea of Duncan asking those questions around the office. I hadn't wanted to believe that he could ever betray me like that. Especially not when I had just gotten back from dealing with one asshole at court.

But I should never have made Abby think I didn't believe her. I should never have let her think, even for a second, that I doubted her judgment.

I felt terrible. Another night that I wished I could take back. I seemed to be having too many of those, ever since I had started things with Abby. I just kept messing up. It was no wonder that she wasn't answering my calls. She wanted nothing to do with me.

I wondered if she was even planning on coming back to work the next day or if that ship had sailed entirely. I felt sick to my stomach just thinking of going back to the office without having her around. Of hiring someone else to be my advisor. I didn't want to hire someone else.

I remembered what Austin had said, when she and I had first started dating. How I was going to have to decide if having a relationship with Abby was worth the potential of losing a great advisor. Suddenly, I was no longer sure.

I just had never pictured things with Abby turning out this wrong. Not in my worst nightmares.

I had holed up in my mansion on Saturday. Safer anyway, I told myself, since there was a gauntlet of paparazzi camped outside the place. Sure, I could have had the police involved, get all of those guys removed. But safer just to stay inside and drink myself to oblivion again.

Of course, that wouldn't work too many days in a row, though. Austin called me on Sunday, letting me know that he was already on his way over. That's what friends were for, I supposed.

I watched from one of the second-story windows as Austin pulled up outside, sending the paparazzi scattering like the bugs that they were. He made his way easily up to the front door, ignoring the questions they flung at him. I headed downstairs in time to hear the noisy chatter from outside before he had fully closed the front door.

He shook his head as he turned to face me. "I think you're more popular than the president," he joked as he kicked off his shoes. He peered at my face. "So how the fuck are you anyway?"

I gave him a look. "How do you think I am?" I asked him.

Austin raised an eyebrow at me. "Dude, I get that the whole trial didn't turn out exactly the way you wanted, but it didn't go too terribly," he said. "The media haven't even been able to come up with a good sound file from it, which I take to mean you didn't say anything too stupid up there." That last was meant as a joke, but I didn't feel like laughing right now.

"Do you want a beer?" I asked over my shoulder, already heading for the kitchen and the waiting fridge.

"Sure," Austin said easily. "So if it's not the trial that has you upset, I'm guessing it's something to do with Abby. Did she panic when she saw how much news coverage the trial got?"

"I don't know," I said sourly.

"Yes, you do," Austin countered, accepting the beer I held out to him. He shook his head. "Come on, Daniel, don't be like that. Just tell me what happened."

Those words reminded me that Austin was my best friend. Maybe my only friend, with the way things had been going lately. Between Ivy sleeping with one of my best friends, my advisor betraying me to the media, and one of my best clients asking inappropriate questions to my staff and generally trying to stir up trouble, it felt like I didn't have a single person in my corner anymore.

Except Abby. She had always been there for me. She had done whatever I asked of her, even taking over as CEO for a few days despite her trepidations that she wasn't prepared for such a role.

And how had I repaid her for her loyalty? With angry words and suspicion.

I stared down at my beer. "Abby and I had a fight," I admitted. "She told one of our clients we would never work with him again. And she had her reasons—all valid ones—but I just wouldn't listen to her. I was so caught up in my own shit. Now she won't return any of my calls, and I don't know what to do." I grimaced. "I get the feeling that if I just showed up at her place, she would slam the door in my face."

Austin shook his head. "That sounds like a mess, man," he said. "Did you find out why she let the client go??"

"He was apparently going around the office asking all the women if they'd ever slept with me," I said bitterly. "You know, just trying to stir up another story for the media." I frowned, suddenly realizing something. "Actually, I wouldn't be surprised if he was somehow in on the plan with Gerrard. They were always chummy in meetings. Gerrard probably told him to come now, while the trial was going on. He couldn't get much money from me for the assault charges, but maybe that was never his target in the first place. He got me out of the office so that his crony could come in and interrogate my staff."

I felt sick just thinking about it. Just when I had thought I was finished with Gerrard, for good. Of course, this was only yet another thing I didn't have solid proof for. I couldn't take Gerrard to court over a suspicion. He would likely go to the grave with all his secrets, and the media would crucify me in the court of public opinion as time went on.

I hated the unfairness of it all. But not as much as I hated the fact that I still didn't know how to clear things up with Abby.

"Are you sure she's not answering your calls because of all of that?" Austin asked carefully.

I blinked at him. "What do you mean?" I asked, wracking my brain for something else I might have done to upset her.

Of course, there was the whole matter of the trial. I knew that she didn't want to be caught up in any of that. Or was she upset that I hadn't let her testify on my behalf? Did she think that that would have swayed the jury so I could have gotten off scot-free? I just didn't want her to feel like she had to get involved. I deserved the consequences of my actions, after all. And she was much more useful around the office.

I had liked knowing she was there. But maybe she felt like I had dismissed her.

Austin clearly had something else in mind, though. He rapidly searched his phone for something. And I could tell from the grim look on his face that I wasn't going to like it. Finally, he found what he was looking for and turned the phone around so that I could see it.

I felt anger course through me when I saw the headline: *Does Abby James Really Know the Man Behind the Smile?* The whole article focused on my past history of "anger issues" and "bar fights." The facts were all true, I'd give them that. There was that time I had been thrown out of Icing for getting into a shouting fight with one of the other guys in the bar, who claimed that I had fouled up his relationship with his girlfriend. And the other time that the bouncer had hauled me out of a place for being too drunk.

I'd been so fucking young at that point, though. If I could just explain all of it to Abby, tell her that none of these pictures or stories were indicative of who I really was.

Austin watched my face as it flipped through a complicated set of emotions. I just didn't know what to say. If this was the reason why Abby wanted nothing to do with me anymore, if she was upset with the fact that I had apparent anger issues, I wasn't sure that there was anything I could do to convince her to come back to me. Or to even listen to me anymore.

Because what could I possibly say to that? It was just like the thing with Gerrard, or this new thing with Duncan. I didn't have any proof of any of it. No proof that I deserved someone like her.

"What are you thinking?" Austin asked warily.

I sighed and shook my head. "I just don't even know what to say," I said. "I really think I've lost her this time, whatever the reason for it. And it hurts. More that I could ever have expected it would."

Austin shook his head. "If you really care about this girl, and I can tell that you do, you'll fight for her," he said confidently.

"How, though?" I asked balefully. "And is that really fair to her anyway? She deserves someone better than me. She doesn't want to be in the media all the time, and she definitely doesn't want to be in the media for things like this. Besides, I told you, I wasn't there for her when she needed my support. I threw her to the wolves, left her alone in the office when she's barely had time to get the hang of the business. I just didn't think of how difficult things could be for her. She's so brilliant that I forget how inexperienced she actually is."

"You could try telling her that," Austin suggested. "I mean, I wouldn't tell her that you think she's inexperienced, because the connotations of that word are pretty terrible. But what if you tell her that she's normally so collected and confident around the office that you forgot that she might need a little advice from you sometimes as well? Or something like that."

I shook my head. "I can't tell her anything like that now," I said. "She won't even answer my calls."

Austin gave me a look. "So what are you going to do, just give up?" he asked. "That's not the Daniel I thought I knew."

I took a healthy swallow of beer, twisting the empty bottle in my hands before chucking it in the recycling bin and moving to grab another one.

"If nothing else," Austin said in a low voice as I closed the fridge, "you have to figure out some better end for the two of you."

"What do you mean?" I asked, staring at the naked refrigerator door in front of me, eyes unseeing.

"I mean that the press thinks the two of you were lovey-dovey and oh-so-happy up until the point that you walked into that trial," Austin said grimly. "You guys break things off now, like this, with no communication whatsoever, and the media will tear the two of you apart. They'll go after Abby for being an idiot and not seeing the signs that you're a terrible guy, and they'll go after you for putting her through all of this. And for just generally being a scumbag."

"Gee, glad to hear what you really think of me," I said sarcastically, yanking the cap off my beer and gulping down at least half of it in one go.

Austin moved around to stand in front of me, prying my beer out of my fingers. "I think you've had enough of that, and enough of self-pity," he said firmly. "Now let's figure out how you're going to fix this. What are your options?"

I sighed. "Go to her house, or wait and see if she shows up to work tomorrow morning."

"I know you," Austin said flatly, "and I know that if you try to wait until work tomorrow before talking to her, it's going to eat you alive." He paused. "It's not healthy to keep all that guilt and anger inside of you. That's how you end up punching out guys like Gerrard in the first place."

I grimaced, but I knew he was probably right. "I'll talk to her," I promised Austin. "But I swear, if I show up at her house and she slams the door in my face, you had better be waiting at your place with all the booze in the world to wash away the rejection."

Austin smiled faintly. "Deal," he said, clapping a hand on my shoulder.

Chapter 14

Abby

FOR THE FIRST TIME in my life, I wasn't exactly looking forward to a family dinner on Sunday evening with Matt, Leanne, and the kids. And I hated that I couldn't feel more enthusiastic about it. The kids were always such rays of sunshine; they could brighten up any day. But it was Leanne and Matt that I was worried about. My brother knew me too well, and my best friend definitely knew me all too well. There was no way that I was getting through this without admitting to the two of them that Daniel and I had had a fight and were now on uncertain terms.

Uncertain, I thought with a snort. Uncertain didn't even begin to cover it.

I had a couple more missed calls from Daniel, but now I was scared to answer for different reasons. If I had just talked things out with him like an adult, maybe we would have been able to salvage our relationship. But as it was, I had run scared. That wasn't an admirable trait. I couldn't blame Daniel if he didn't want to see me ever again.

Logically, I knew that Daniel wasn't looking for reasons to dump me, but I just couldn't seem to quit compiling a list of all the reasons why he would never want to see me again. I had screwed up at work, I had listened to the tabloid stories about him even for a moment, I hadn't let him explain his side of things even as I was yelling at him to stop yelling at me and listen to what I had to say. What a freakin' mess.

When I got to Matt and Leanne's, I paused on the doorstep for a moment. Normally, I would ring the bell and wait for someone to open it. Even though Matt and I had grown up together in this house, it now felt very much like his and Leanne's. Matt always told me that I was crazy, but maybe I had to distance myself from the way that the house had been.

The thought of distancing myself physically hurt me. That was what I was going to have to do with Daniel, if I went back to work for him the following day. Could I ever really do that? I had a hard time believing I could.

Daniel probably wouldn't want me around anyway. It was his office and his employees. I had been the one to jeopardize the comfortable ecosystem of McGregor Enterprises. Daniel would fire me, and I'd lose the one job I had ever really enjoyed having.

I swallowed hard. Maybe that was for the best.

I had to stop thinking about all of that, anyway. I tried to paste a smile on my face but was only moderately successful. Then, I opened the front door and slipped inside without knocking. It was probably a dead giveaway to the fact that I wasn't feeling great mentally that day, but I figured if I could find the kids first and play with them some before I even had to see Matt and Leanne, maybe I could get a better mood solidly in place so that they wouldn't question me.

When I got into the living room, though, following the sounds of Zach's voice, I found that Matt was down on the carpet playing cars with his two children. He glanced up at me and grinned. For a second, I saw the flicker of a frown on his face, and I knew that whatever smile I had shown him, it hadn't been convincing. But then, he was scooting over on the floor to make space for me.

"Which car do you want?" he asked me.

I slowly sank down next to him. "You must be feeling better," I said. Matt had been pretty lucky with his accident, all things considered. Some asshole had run a red light and crashed sidelong into Matt's car, crumpling the whole thing. He'd ended up having to go into surgery due to internal bleeding, and he'd been moving pretty slowly ever since.

This was the first time I'd seen him down on the floor playing with the kids since then.

I hadn't realized how good it was to see him feeling better again. Matt was normally so vivacious and charismatic that seeing him in the hospital, half asleep and in pain, weak and pale, had been a shock to the system for sure. This made things seem normal again.

I just wished I could be in a better mood to actually enjoy the change.

We played with the cars for a while, zooming them around the whole living room while Zach narrated the action excitedly. Normally, I'd be making up funny commentary of my own to add to his, but tonight, I just couldn't get into the game. Finally, Leanne poked her head into the living room and told the kids to go wash up. They darted off, and I started to follow them. But Matt caught my wrist before I could go.

"Is everything okay?" he asked, his eyes searching my face.

I tried that fake smile again, but it felt brittle. "Sure," I told him. But when I saw the way his eyebrows knit together, I sighed, knowing I needed to come clean about everything. It would probably make me feel better to confide in someone, anyway. "Daniel and I had a fight. And I don't need you to tell me that you told me so, but I guess he just wasn't the guy I thought he was."

Matt shook his head. "I would never say I told you so over something like that," he said gravely. "What do you mean, though? What happened?"

"I made a mistake at work," I finally confessed. "When I was standing in for him as CEO, during the trial. It doesn't matter what it was. I don't really want to talk about it. But anyway, I made a mistake."

"What did Daniel say?" Matt growled, and I could hear the protective edge to his voice.

"It wasn't so much what he said." I sighed. "It was more just that he yelled at me. I already felt stupid enough about making such a rookie mistake and overstepping my role. But then to have him yell at me on top of that, I don't know. I knew that I wasn't ready to take over for him as CEO, even temporarily, and I guess the only way that I had convinced myself that it would be okay was because I told myself he would cut me some slack. But then he didn't."

"That's such bullshit," Matt said, shaking his head.

I shook my own head. "I don't know if it is," I said. "That's sort of the way that things happen in the business world, Matt. It has to be. Mistakes in business can cost a company tons of money, or employees."

"I'm sorry, but if you're telling me that Daniel favors his company over you, then he's more of an asshole than I thought," Matt said succinctly. He paused and then shook his head. "But to be honest, I just don't see that. I've seen the way the guy looks at you. And the way he talks about you, as well as to you. The guy's head over heels for you."

I shrugged. "So what?" I asked unhappily. "I should just give him a free pass to yell at me whenever he wants to?" I shook my head. "It just seems like there's a pattern there. Punching Gerrard at the bar, yelling at me now. I don't know what else he's done; the internet has a thousand stories, but I'm just not sure he's the kind of guy I really want to be with."

Matt was frowning, but I could practically see the gears turning in his head as he carefully selected his next words. "This trial couldn't have been easy for Daniel," he said finally. "I'm not sure that yelling at you is establishing any sort of pattern of anger; I'd say that it's probably more that he's been under a lot of pressure between the trial and work, then unhappy with the way that things went. And he lashed out at you. It's not fair at all, but sometimes, people can't help it."

"I'm surprised to hear you defend him," I told Matt. Because even though he and Leanne had come around to Daniel at the hospital, thanks to how helpful he had made himself during that hard time, I still had sort of expected both Matt and Leanne to say good riddance when they found out about the fight.

Matt shrugged at me. "Abby, I can tell how happy he makes you. And like I said, it's easy to see that he adores you. I'm not saying that the guy is perfect or that you're wrong. I'm just saying that if you haven't already talked to the guy again since you had your fight—and I know you well enough to know that you probably haven't—you should at least give him a chance to explain himself." He grinned at me. "I'm sure you know exactly how many stupid things I've said to Leanne over the years. We've had our fights."

"I know," I said. The two of them were good about not coming to me during their fights, realizing how awkward it would be for me to be caught in the middle of the two of them. But Leanne had told me about a few of them afterward, when their tempers had both cooled off a little. I knew how much work it took to maintain a relationship.

Wasn't that something I had reminded Daniel of, once upon a time when we were first starting this thing? That the relationship would be work and that we were going to have to put in some effort to try to make things okay between us? Maybe I really was just running scared.

My phone rang, as though I had summoned his call with my thoughts. I glanced down at it. Daniel again.

I knew that Matt was right, that I needed to talk to him and at least hear what he had to say. If he wanted to fire me, then so be it. But maybe he just really wanted to apologize. If so, it wasn't fair for me to continue ignoring him.

I thought back to that text message he had already sent me, in which he had already apologized. Suddenly, I felt horribly guilty, knowing that I should have called him back sooner, no matter my myriad reasons for not doing so. They were all just excuses. I was so afraid of falling for the wrong guy again that as soon as I had an excuse, I ran.

"Is that him?" Matt asked.

I nodded. Then, I sighed. "You're right," I allowed. "I need to talk to him. To at least give him a chance to say whatever it is that he wants to say. Then I can make my decisions from there."

Matt nodded approvingly. "If you want some privacy, the kids are probably already at the table, and I'll join them and let Leanne know what's up."

I shook my head, knowing that I was chickening out again but unable to help it. "Nah, let's just have dinner," I said. "I don't want to disrupt the whole night. But I'll call him back later."

"If you're sure," Matt said, nodding at me.

We headed into the kitchen and found that Leanne had already gotten the kids started on their dinner of chicken nuggets and mac 'n' cheese, plus plated out food for the grown-ups. "Everything okay?" she asked, giving her husband a worried and quizzical look.

"I'm fine," Matt told her gently, squeezing her shoulder as he passed her to sit in his normal seat. I realized she must have been worried about him, thinking that maybe it was something to do with his injuries. Instead, it was just my drama all over again.

I was hating how much drama there was in my life, ever since I started dating Daniel. But suddenly, I realized that I was the cause of at least as much of that drama as Daniel was. After all, I had been the one to break things off with him the first time, and I had been the one who refused to even talk to him this weekend, all because we'd had a little fight.

And as I looked around the table at Matt and Leanne, as I listened to Zach and Layla tell me all about their week at school and everything else that they had gotten up to, I realized suddenly that I wanted this. All of it, the whole package. I had never really thought that I might want children. Or rather, I had been sure that I would never find a man that I wanted children with.

Daniel might have his faults, but I knew, deep down, that in spite of everything, he was a great guy. Not perfect, but not some terrible asshole with anger management issues either. I had only seen him raise his voice twice, once at the bar with Gerrard and once toward me. That really wasn't all that much in the scheme of things. Not only that, but

Erin had seemed sure that Gerrard deserved a good punch to the face, and maybe she was right.

Maybe I had never given Daniel a chance to tell me his side of the story. Maybe I had been in the wrong all along.

I could still picture a future with Daniel. More easily than I could picture a future without him. I could see him and I together at the dinner table, could see him laughing as the children complained about the broccoli on their plates. We'd fall asleep together every night, and in the morning, he would get the coffee and breakfast going while I got the kids ready for school.

It definitely felt like it was too soon to be having these sorts of thoughts about Daniel. But then again, when I thought back to all the changes that had happened since I had started working for McGregor Enterprises, it felt as though I had known Daniel a lot better than I really could. And maybe it was just that I was used to reading people in business, but I really felt like I knew Daniel.

Better than the tabloids ever could. Better than that jury had, for sure.

I winced when I thought about the jury. Daniel had been on trial for two days, listening to people who believed he was a terrible person, and when he had come home to me, clearly needing some assurance that he wasn't, I had run away. I felt terrible about that now.

I'd call him immediately after dinner, I vowed. Right after dinner.

Chapter 15

Daniel

I DIDN'T KNOW WHAT to do. I had gotten it in my head, after talking to Austin, that I would talk to Abby before work tomorrow morning. With it in my head, it was even more difficult to stomach the silence from her. I had to apologize to her. I had to make sure she knew what she meant to me. How much I appreciated her work around the office. She hadn't had to step in for me as CEO, but she had done so. And she had done a damned good job of it, I was sure, the whole thing with Duncan aside.

I never should have yelled at her. And I never should have let it go this long without apologizing to her, even though it was sort of her fault for not answering her phone.

She still wasn't answering her phone, and when I went by her apartment, she didn't answer the door. I stood out there for a moment, indecision in every part of my body.

Maybe she was over at Matt and Leanne's house. It would make sense for her to go there if she was upset. It was about dinnertime right now, and I knew she and her brother and best friend had dinner together regularly.

Even if she wasn't there, maybe I could ask Matt for advice. I felt kind of weird going to him for advice since I knew that neither he nor Leanne had really been happy with me dating Abby to begin with. But if anyone knew Abby well enough to give me advice, it was Matt. And right now, I could use all the advice I could get.

I wasn't ready to lose her from my life; I didn't think I would ever be ready to lose her from my life. But with the way she was ignoring me right now, not even bothering to text me back and tell me that she never wanted to see me again or anything else, I couldn't help but feel worried. Maybe she wouldn't show up to work tomorrow. Maybe I would never see or hear from her again.

I couldn't handle that. I needed Matt's advice, if that was what she planned to do.

I had been to dinner once at Matt and Leanne's house, and it didn't take long for me to drive over there again. When I pulled in the driveway, I sighed with relief to see Abby's car parked outside. I had made the right decision, then.

I hoped so, anyway. I hoped she wouldn't be mad at me for just showing up like this.

I swallowed hard, drumming my fingers against the edge of the steering wheel for a moment, further indecision coursing through my body. Maybe I should just leave it for later. Let her have the evening she had planned with her brother and his family. I didn't want to intrude. I didn't want to cause any more drama in her life.

But at the same time, could it wait until later? Tomorrow morning, Abby was theoretically supposed to come to work at McGregor Enterprises, just like usual. And I'd be back at work after the trial with Gerrard. There was no way for the two of us to avoid seeing each other. And if she wasn't planning on being there, in light of the fight that she and I had, I deserved to know that before she just didn't show up. Or called in sick, or whatever she might be tempted to do.

Because then I would have to call her back, and this rejection wasn't something I wanted to handle over the phone. We owed it to each other, and to ourselves, to have this conversation face-to-face, like adults.

I took a final deep breath and got out of the car, then walked briskly toward the front door. I knocked softly, aware of the fact that the kids were probably there at the dinner table with them. If the door was going to get slammed in my face, I didn't want them to get suspicious. I didn't want to cause any more pain than I had to.

It was Matt who answered the door. I could see the look of surprise on his face, and I didn't miss the way he raised an eyebrow at me. But he nodded warmly at me and stood back to let me inside. "I'll go get Abby," he said, slipping away toward the kitchen. I didn't try to follow him. Instead, I waited in the front hall, rocking back and forth on my heels.

When Abby came out into the hall, I expected her to look just as surprised. Or maybe furious at the way I had just shown up here. But instead, she looked resigned. "Daniel," she said curtly.

I grimaced, already hating the emotions I could see in her face. She was closed off, impassive. Like she didn't care about me at all, and in fact like she had never cared about me at all. I stared at her for a long moment, but her expression didn't change, and she didn't say anything. Finally, I sighed. "Sorry, I think I made a mistake in coming here," I told her. "I should have just texted. But I just wanted to know what you planned on doing about tomorrow. If you still planned on showing up at work."

Abby gave me a considering look, but she still looked somehow detached from all of this, like she didn't really care at all. She gave me a nod at last. "Yeah, I'll be there," she said. "I guess we need to talk, though. About how we're going to handle all of this."

"I'm sorry," I blurted in response. "I'm sorry for how I acted. I didn't mean to push you away, and I definitely didn't mean to hurt your feelings. I know you did the best that you could as interim CEO, and actually you did an amazing job. In spite of the fact that you've only been with the company for a short time, and in spite of the fact that I gave you barely any time to consider it and barely any time to prepare for it. I'm so proud of what you accomplished, I can't even tell you. And I didn't tell you that before. And I'm sorry."

The words all sounded so lame as they spilled from my mouth, but was it just my imagination or was Abby warming up to my being there? Her expression was no longer quite as frosty, and she was clearly paying attention to every word I said, rather than glancing back over her shoulder toward the kitchen like she had been doing. It no longer looked quite so much like she wanted to bolt.

"I was overwhelmed," I continued. "And that's absolutely no excuse for my inability to control my emotions. I do know that I never should have yelled at you like that or said any of the things I did. Like I told you, I probably would have done exactly the same thing if our positions had been reversed. If I had been the one dealing with Duncan." I shook my head. "I never should have yelled at you," I repeated, feeling even more ridiculous as I repeated myself.

Abby frowned at me, but finally she nodded. "It's all right," she said slowly.

I shook my head again, though. "No, it isn't," I told her. "It's not all right at all."

Abby stared at me for a moment and then let out a short, bitter laugh. "Daniel, I wanted to have this conversation. I wanted to hear your side of the story. But let's be realistic here. There are a dozen ways I messed up."

"You told me that you didn't want to be in the public eye, and I put you there front and center," I interrupted, ticking off my own mistakes on my fingertips. "Hell, I got served for assault charges in the first place. And I gave you no warning on taking over for me. And I left you a fucking mountain of paperwork in the office as if *that* would help you with anything, rather than just stressing you out. And I—"

Abby held up both hands, her lips twitching with what I was sure was amusement. "All right, all right," she said. "So we agree that we were both wrong?"

I gave her a serious look. "We agree that no matter what I did wrong, or what you imagine you did wrong, our fight the other day was wrong," I corrected. "Because forgetting about all the rest of it, and even factoring in all the stress I was under? That was no way to talk to the woman that I love."

The words were out of me before I could even think about them, but I knew they were right just then. I loved Abby. Maybe she hadn't worked for me so long, and maybe there was still a lot we needed to get through. But at the end of the day, I loved her, and that right there was the reason that losing her, in my personal life as well as around the office, worried me.

At the end of the day, I loved her. And that was all there was to it.

"You love me?" Abby asked in surprise. Then, her face fell a little. "You mean, as your advisor." Her words were flat and disheartened.

I frowned, my arms itching to reach for her, to pull her towards me, to use physical touch to ease all her worries. But I didn't want to overstep. Not until I fully understood what she was feeling. So instead, I shook my head. "No," I told her. "Not just as my advisor. Abby, I love you. And I'm sorry that I've done a piss-poor job of showing you how amazing I really think you are, but I am hoping you give me one more chance. Even though I know that by all rights, I don't deserve it."

Chapter 16

Abby

I STARED AT DANIEL, wondering just what to say in response to that declaration of love. Of course, it didn't solve everything. I wasn't the kind of woman who believed that just because a man told me he loved me, suddenly everything was going to be all roses and chocolate kisses. Love didn't solve things at work, or the media, or the anger issues. Love didn't make up for all the ways I had messed up as well.

But then again, I had never even expected Daniel to just show up like this. His phone calls, sure—after the way he had been calling me, I had expected there would still be some kind of conversation. Maybe over the phone, or maybe at work tomorrow. But to just show up at Matt's house in the middle of dinner? That was...different. And there was something about it that made me feel somehow both worse and better.

He cared enough to be there. Like he thought all of this was his fault. I was glad that he could admit his actions weren't entirely correct. It also made me feel worse for not answering any of his calls.

But he didn't seem like he was here just to hash out the blame over all of that. No, it seemed like he was here because he really wanted to fix things between the two of us. I didn't know just what to say in response to that.

Finally, I sighed and looked away from his earnest face. "I'll see you tomorrow morning," I promised him. Because it had never really been a question of whether or not I was continuing to work for him. I liked the job, and even though I knew I had messed things up in my time as a

CEO, I felt sure that I could recover when I went back to being just his advisor again.

At least, if everyone around the office was as forgiving as Daniel was. And if he and I didn't show up to work together the following morning, putting the exclamation point on whatever stories the media had spent the weekend coming up with, thanks to whatever dirt Duncan had uncovered.

Was there any dirt there? I hated that I still had to think about that.

"Is this a routine for you?" I suddenly blurted out.

Daniel looked confused for a second. "Showing up to..." Then he trailed off, comprehension dawning. "Sleeping with people around the office," he said flatly.

"I hate that I have to ask," I hurried to say. "And I don't feel like I really need to ask. First of all, it's not really any of my business who you've slept with before. And second of all, I don't really believe that you have, despite everything I've ever heard about you, and despite all the unwarranted advice that everyone has tried to give me about this whole thing." I was gesturing awkwardly between the two of us, I realized.

I took a deep breath, bringing my hands back down to my sides. "It's just that I don't know what to expect from you or the media. Or from Duncan now, for that matter. And that's terrifying, honestly. Because I want to believe that you're the guy I know you are, the guy I've seen ever since I started working for McGregor Enterprises. But I also don't want to look like an idiot defending you if it turns out you're not the man I thought you were."

Daniel gave me half a smile. "I'm not even sure I know what you're saying anymore," he joked.

"I'm trying to say that I love you as well, you idiot," I said matter-of-factly. "So you'd better tell me now if there's any reason why I shouldn't."

The words were surprisingly easy, now that I gave myself subconscious permission to say them. And you would have thought it was the worst possible time to say them. If I was waiting for the romantic time to blurt out declarations of love, I surely should have kept waiting. But there was something about Daniel's facial expression that let me know just how worried he was that he was losing me. And that in itself made me want to do everything in my power to reassure him he still had me.

That he had captured me, heart and soul; that no matter what he did, or I did, I would keep coming back to him, if he would only let me.

Daniel stared at me for a beat longer and then took a step closer, cupping my cheeks between his palms, kissing me gently. He pulled back, brushing his thumb along my cheekbone. "I know that kisses can't make everything right between us," he said. "But I just can't help myself."

I laughed, unable to help it. "Kisses are all right," I said, leaning up on my toes to kiss him again until we were both breathless this time. When I pulled away from the kiss, I still leaned into his body. "I know you had a lot on your mind," I told him. "And I wish there were something that I could do to make the Duncan situation better. I really am sorry about that."

Daniel shook his head, leaning his forehead against mine. "Forget about that," he said, brushing my hair back behind my ear, his fingers lingering there for a moment. He sighed and pulled away. "We have a lot to talk about. But just promise me that we will talk and that you won't keep shutting me out like this. This weekend has been hard, I have to admit."

"It's been hard for me, too," I said softly. "But I promise I won't keep ignoring you."

Matt cleared his throat from nearby, before Daniel could lean in to kiss me again or vice versa. I blushed brilliantly, pulling away. What my brother must be thinking right now? I had told him that Daniel and

I would talk, of course, and Matt had been the one to convince me of that. He had told me that he believed Daniel was a good guy.

But all the same, I felt embarrassed, almost, that I had caved so easily. A few gentle words, and here I was, ready to get in over my head again. I supposed that was another thing I needed to talk to Daniel about. This getting in over my head thing, I couldn't keep doing that. It was what had undone us the first time, because I'd panicked about the media coverage. I knew better than to do that again.

Except that with all the drama I'd been through, I still wanted Daniel. And I knew that I would regardless of what happened. It was the only reason that I'd been willing to let the press know about us in the first place. I trusted Daniel. And I trusted that he wasn't making drama because he wanted to.

All media things aside, he needed someone by his side, just like I did. And it wouldn't be fair to leave him on his own just because I was nervous that one day he might want to leave me.

"Leanne's putting the kids to bed in a minute," Matt told us. "How about the two of you come into the living room for a glass of wine?"

I knew immediately what he was trying to do: get us out of the hallway, where the kids would have to pass us on their way upstairs, as well as getting Daniel further inside, where he and I would have no choice but to talk, where Matt and Daniel could talk as well.

But Matt didn't ask any of the horrible questions I imagined as we headed into the living room. Instead, he poured us each a glass of a nice red cabernet and sat us down in the cozy living room. "How've you been, Daniel?" he asked easily.

Daniel made a face and then glanced over at me, like he was wondering just how much I had already told my brother. "I'm sure you've seen the news," he finally said.

"Some of it," Matt agreed, shrugging. "And I'm sure the trial sucked. But that's not exactly what I asked." There was the hint of a smile at the corners of his lips, and I suddenly realized that Matt was teasing Daniel.

And wasn't that the surest sign I could get that Matt and Leanne had accepted Daniel?

Daniel glanced over at me. "Things are okay," he finally said. "Not great, but okay."

Matt grinned at him and then transferred his grin to me. "I know that feeling," he said. "What happens now?"

"What do you mean?" Daniel asked in surprise.

"Now that you're done with the trial," Matt clarified. "What happens next?"

Daniel shrugged one shoulder. "I guess I go back to work as usual," he said, with another glance over at me. "That is, as long as Abby is willing to come back to work as my advisor. Otherwise, I guess what happens is that I have to start interviewing for someone new. But that's not what I really want to be doing."

Matt snorted, and Leanne, as she entered the room, started laughing. Daniel grinned at them. "The thing is, this trial didn't turn out as badly as it could have. They slammed me with the maximum fine, but not to sound like an ass, that money is nothing to me. As for the anger management courses, well." He looked over at me, raw honesty in his gaze. "I'm still not sure that I really need them, but they can only help, right?"

I smiled back at him and reached over to rest a hand on his thigh, squeezing lightly.

"And the two of you are doing all right?" Leanne asked carefully, her eyes full of concern as she looked over at me. I knew I probably hadn't been subtle about my mood through dinner, and I wondered how much Matt had filled her in on while I was out of the room. Not that I really minded. When it really came down to it, the only reason I had held off on telling Leanne about this was that I wanted to do some thinking of my own before asking her opinion, and I felt embarrassed about the mistake I had made. Daniel and Matt had helped me feel less embarrassed about the whole thing, and now I was just glad that things seemed to be okay between the two of us.

Daniel had even said that he loved me. Not in the heat of passion, but he had just said it, like it was fact.

"We're doing all right," Daniel said, and I realized that everyone had been waiting for me to answer Leanne's question. But while I thought about our earlier conversation, Daniel answered effortlessly. It made relief rush through me. We really were okay, then. He wasn't mad at me. I hadn't lost him.

"Actually," Daniel continued, glancing over at me, "one of my top priorities going back to work will be training Abby up to be a CEO."

I stared at him in surprise. "You don't have to do that," I protested.

Daniel rolled his eyes as he grinned at me. "Of course I don't have to," he said. "And don't make the mistake of thinking that I'm excited for the day you quit your job as my advisor so that you can take a CEO position with some other company. But I think it'll be good for you."

I grimaced. "Because then the next time you need me to step in and help out, I won't make such a stupid mistake?" I guessed.

"Of course not," Daniel said, shaking his head. "Come on, like I said, I would probably have done the same thing with Duncan. You need to quit beating yourself up over that. But I do think that a little more training will make you feel more comfortable if you need to take over for me again. I know this time was probably a bit overwhelming. This will make things better for both of us."

"I don't know if I'm really ready to start training to be a CEO yet," I said, frowning. "That's a lot of responsibility. And I feel like I'm only just starting to get a handle on the rest of my duties as your advisor."

Daniel laughed. "I don't plan on heaping responsibilities on you," he said. "As you know, I hate delegating much of anything anyway. And if I make things too difficult for you, all you have to do is let me know and we'll scale things back. But put it this way: I threw you into the thick of things and you handled yourself beautifully. I don't really think you're going to have any trouble."

And with the way he smiled at me, I was sure he was right. He'd be there to coach me every step of the way. This was just training; the stakes wouldn't be nearly as high as they'd been over the couple days of the trial when I'd had to cover for him. Not only that, but he was still so sure that I could do this.

I nodded at him. "All right," I said. "If you think that's for the best."

"I'm still just glad that everything worked out all right with the trial," Leanne said. "And that things worked out for you, Abby, in your trial as CEO of the company."

I reached over and caught Daniel's hand, smiling at Matt and Leanne. "I'm just glad that you had me over for dinner tonight," I joked. "That was probably the best meal I've had in a while."

There was laughter all around, and the conversation turned to lighter topics from there.

Daniel and I might still have more to discuss, but suddenly, all my worries of the past few days seemed so silly. Daniel would never hurt me, and just because he'd yelled at me, it didn't mean that he suddenly hated me. Hell, he didn't even want to fire me. I had to calm down about this relationship.

Daniel wasn't like my exes—I just had to remember that. Let him show me the person he really was. Stop running away from this.

I smiled over at him, and he squeezed my hand. "I guess I should get going," he said to Leanne and Matt, an apologetic note in his voice. "I want to get to work early tomorrow morning so I can get caught up on everything that happened while I was gone." He glanced over at me. "I want to talk to Erin, in particular, about what Duncan did. I might see if there's any sort of legal action we can take against him. Asking about my workers' sex lives has to count as harassment or something."

I frowned. "I feel like the press would be all over that, though. You step out of the office for two days and suddenly you're back in the courtroom, this time as the prosecution?"

"True, true," Daniel said, nodding at me. "We'll talk about it before I do anything, I promise you. But I still want to talk to Erin and some of the other women first, just to get their side of the story and all of the specifics."

A couple days ago, I might have been offended, but now I knew he wasn't saying that because he didn't believe my account. He was the CEO of the business, and he had to know everything that had happened on Friday. So I simply nodded at him.

I looked back at my brother and my best friend. "I guess that means I should be leaving as well. Can't let this guy beat me to the office in the morning," I joked.

"After the work you put in last week, you're welcome to take the day off," Daniel said, but I could tell from his tone that he was reluctant not to see me the next day. I appreciated his offer, but I shook my head.

"Nah, I'll be there. No one better to get you all caught up on what you missed."

"True," Daniel said, nodding at me.

We both stood up and, after the goodbyes were said, headed for the door.

Chapter 17

Daniel

AS WE WALKED OUTSIDE, I couldn't resist the urge to put an arm around Abby's lower back, drawing her in closer to me. I was so glad that everything seemed to be resolved between the two of us. I couldn't bear the thought of losing her. But it sounded like she appreciated my apology and was ready to look forward.

I knew I was going to see her at work the next morning, but I found myself hating the moment I had to pull away from her tonight. I'd missed her over this long weekend of not talking. Not only that, but we had both admitted that we loved the other tonight. It felt like leaving now was leaving things unsaid.

I wanted her to know how grateful I really was to have her in my life.

I spun her around toward me and kissed her gently. Abby leaned into me, her fingers twisting in the front of my shirt as she fought to keep her balance.

"Why don't you let me drive you home?" I asked her, my lips still close to hers, close enough that I could feel her breath against my skin. It woke a fire in my groin, my body automatically pressing closer to hers.

Abby grinned against my lips. "Thought we needed to get home so that we could get to work early tomorrow morning," she said. "Or are you telling me that you dragged me away from my brother and friend so that we could have sex?"

"As long as we're in bed, it counts as resting, doesn't it?" I joked.

Abby laughed and pulled away, regret in her eyes. "But I actually drove here this time, rather than taking an Uber," she said, gesturing toward her vehicle.

I rolled my eyes. "I'm sure Matt and Leanne won't mind if you leave it here overnight. I'll send someone to pick it up tomorrow and have it brought to your home. Or to work, whichever you'd prefer."

Abby grinned at me. "The perks of having a billionaire boyfriend," she teased.

"Guess so," I said, grinning right back at her. "Does that mean yes?"

"Yes," Abby said, nodding her head and following me to my car.

We got in, and I pulled out of the driveway. "Listen, Abby," I began, but Abby held up one hand.

"We've apologized enough," she said. "Let's not worry about it anymore."

I smiled at her. "Sounds like a plan," I said. "But tomorrow, I do want you to come in to work with me. If the media have already talked to Duncan and want to ask you anything, I want to be there to fend them off."

"Agreed," Abby said, nodding.

I reached over and put a hand on her inner thigh, rubbing small circles there with my thumb. "I missed you," I told her.

Abby rolled her eyes comically. "You're such a girl," she joked. "I can't believe that hasn't been in the tabloids yet, that Daniel McGregor is such a romantic."

I snorted. "I'm different with you than I've ever been with anyone before," I told her, thinking about the relationship I'd had with Ivy. "Even with my ex, I don't know. She didn't inspire protectiveness or romantic gestures. I guess that's partly because she just liked being the center of attention. She wanted the media's eyes on her all the time."

Abby made a face. "Yeah, I can't even imagine," she said. "The less the media knows about me, the better."

We fell silent for a bit. I still couldn't stop thinking about how different this relationship with Abby was from my relationship with Ivy. I had thought that I loved Ivy, but now I had to wonder. Maybe I had just loved the idea of being in love with Ivy. Maybe I had just loved the future we would have been able to build together.

That whole relationship, it had felt like I was trying so hard. Like there was thought involved in loving her. But with Abby, I didn't have to think at all. I just knew I loved her. The words had slipped out so easily tonight, and I could tell as soon as I'd said them that Abby loved me as well. I just knew that, too.

It didn't mean that we were destined to be together forever. I knew that I would have to work to keep my promises. Prove to her what a good man I could be, keep her out of the media's eyes as much as I could. It was always possible that it wouldn't be enough, that things would be too difficult and that we would need to step back from each other again.

But I also knew that if we were both willing to put in the work, we could have an amazing future together. Move in together, build a home, maybe start a family. I wanted that more than I could believe.

When I glanced over at Abby, I saw that her eyes were closed. I had to smile at that. She had looked tired when I'd seen her in the light at Matt's place. Maybe this weekend had been just as difficult for her as it had been for me. I didn't like the idea that I had caused her any sort of pain, but at the same time, it was nice to have that realization that she cared about me just as much as I cared about her.

I was still a little worried about how much I did care for her. I couldn't remember what the point of my life had been before her. Now, it seemed like all my energy was turned toward building a better relationship with her. I still went to work, did everything I needed to do. I wasn't shirking my responsibilities. But work didn't seem to have the meaning that it had once had.

That was frightening, honestly. If I did lose Abby, I didn't know what I would do. Go on a bender, probably. Destroy everything I had ever worked for? I doubted it, but it definitely did feel like I was in over my head.

It was exhilarating in some ways, this risk. But terrifying as well.

I'd just have to make sure I didn't do anything that would make her hate me.

I thought about taking her back home to her place. When things had been going well between the two of us, she had stayed over at my place pretty much every night. She even had some of her things there. But with the way that things had been lately, I didn't want to presume, and we hadn't really clarified when I had asked if I could take her home.

But if I was going to be bringing her in to work in the morning, which wasn't too far away even now, then it made more sense just to bring her back to my place. If she didn't want to share a bed with me, she could stay in one of the guest rooms. She'd still have that choice. And I didn't like the idea of going home alone right now.

Besides, I didn't want her to think that I didn't want to sleep with her, that I didn't want to bring her back to my place. That wasn't it at all. I just wanted her to be comfortable.

I made a split-second decision and turned the car toward my place on the far end of town. Abby was still sleeping when I got there, and I spared a moment to smile over at her after I shut off the car. I slipped quietly out of the car and came around to her side. She slumbered on as I opened the door, so I lifted her carefully out of the car, kicking the door shut and carrying her to the house.

Her eyes flickered open as I jostled her slightly in the process of getting the door open. She looked bemused for a second, and then she smiled beatifically at me. "Hey," she said.

I grinned at her. "Hey, sleepyhead," I said, carrying her inside. "Sorry to wake you."

"You can put me down," Abby said. "I can walk."

I shrugged as much as I could with her in my arms, carrying her carefully upstairs. "My room or guest room?" I asked.

Abby stared at me for a moment and then nuzzled against my chest, her fingers twisting in my shirt again. "Yours," she said softly, peeking up at me through her lashes. "If that's okay?"

I smiled down at her. "Of course it is," I told her, carrying her to my room. I set her down on the edge of the bed and knelt to remove her shoes.

She laughingly pushed me away, wakefulness coming back into her eyes. "Don't be silly," she said.

"Taking care of you is silly?" I asked.

"No, but stripping me down is, when you could be stripping yourself," Abby said, eyeing me meaningfully. "And the sooner we're both naked, the sooner we can get in bed and...rest." I didn't miss the pause before the final word, and I knew she had more in mind than just resting.

I grinned at her and starting unbuttoning my shirt, not missing the way that her eyes darkened with lust. She watched as I stripped out of my clothes, letting them fall to the floor, and I groaned, giving my member a few quick strokes just to take the edge off, unable to help myself. I was fully hard already, no doubt partly because my body had become so used to having her naked body pressed against mine every night.

Abby raised an eyebrow at me. "Did you miss me?" she asked teasingly, accurately guessing my thoughts.

"Course I did," I said, coming over to the bed and covering her body with mine. I kissed her tenderly. "I really am sorry about the fight, and about putting you in a situation you were uncomfortable with," I murmured as we broke apart. "I know you said that we should stop apologizing, but I just want to make sure you really know just how sorry I am."

"Show me," Abby challenged, her eyes glinting with excitement.

"Show you?" I asked. I grinned at her and slowly trailed kisses along her skin, until she was shivering beneath me. I trailed my fingers through the slick, velvety cleft between her legs, thumbing at her clit even as my mouth found its way to her left breast, licking and sucking at the nipple until it stood out from her dusky areola.

I pushed two fingers inside of her, eyes never leaving her face. Her fingers twisted in the sheets, and she arched her back, trying to get me deeper inside of her. Slowly, I started to work my fingers, surprised at how slick she already was. Like her body had been waiting just as restlessly to come back to me, same as I'd been feeling.

I kissed lower, lightly tugging at the skin of her navel with my teeth. I could see the trail of goose bumps on her skin, could feel them against my lips as I moved ever lower, trailing kisses on the inside of her thigh while her legs fell helplessly open to me.

Even as I moved my lips and tongue down her body, I continued to press my fingers in and out of her warm hole, feeling her walls contracting against me already, trying to draw me further into her. I could tell the exact moment when my fingers alone ceased to be enough, could hear it in the soft moan she made, could tell she was one breath away from begging.

I moved before she could, tonguing at her slit as my fingers moved to play with her clit. She shuddered, her knees fluttering in and out, and I knew that I had her already, before I had even entered her with my throbbing cock. I grinned against her soft and sensitive skin, still plunging my tongue in and out of her quivering hole.

As she fell back against the bed, I moved back up her body, palming myself with a few quick strokes. That was all that it took for me to be ready against her entrance. "This okay?" I asked quietly.

Abby's eyes flew open, her hips squirming. "Please," she said breathlessly.

I brushed her hair back, fingers lingering tenderly on her cheek before I leaned in to kiss her. Our tongues met as I thrust my rod inside of her waiting cavern, seating myself fully inside of her. She turned her head to the side and gasped for air, hips already moving against mine, fingers seeking purchase against my back.

We moved together, a slow and even rocking motion. She whimpered, her head falling back against the pillows, inviting me to kiss my way back down the long column of her neck. I ran my fingers down her sides, bringing up more goose bumps on her soft skin. I could feel my orgasm building and could tell that she was nearing another as well, but I didn't want to cum just yet. I wanted this to last. Forever, if we could have that.

So I slowed my thrusts further, making her really work to get me fully inside of her, then pulling out nearly all the way before I pushed back in again. She sobbed with need, and I panted for breath, overcome by how perfect this was.

It couldn't last forever, though, as it turned out. My hips began to pick up speed, moving on their own without conscious direction from my brain. I was so far gone already, caught up in the scent of her, in the feeling of her beautiful body against mine. There was nothing in this world except for us, except for me showing her how sorry I was, showing her how much I cared about her, how much I loved her.

I loved her. So simple, so easy, no thinking required. I loved her. I knew it in my bones.

I groaned as I climaxed, balls tight and dick twitching as I buried myself in her one final time. She came at the same time, practically screaming as pleasure poured through her body. She clung to me, and I fell against her, mindful not to crush her but barely able to support myself as my strength poured out of me and into her.

I sucked in a deep breath and pulled out, rolling to the side and falling on my back. Then, grinning, I reached out a hand to trail my fingers down Abby's side. She shivered, body still overcome with the force of her orgasm, and then rolled toward me, putting her head on my chest. I wrapped my arms around her.

We were both asleep before I could think another thought.

Chapter 18

Abby

EVEN WITHOUT AN ALARM, I woke up early on Monday morning, feeling refreshed. It made sense: I hadn't slept well over the weekend, too worried about work and things with Daniel. Now that all of that was resolved, I could catch up on the sleep I'd been missing.

Plus, there was something to be said for having Daniel's arms wrapped comfortably around my body.

I smiled as I came into full awareness, rubbing my palm down Daniel's arm. He kissed the back of my neck, his body pressing closer against mine. "You awake?" he murmured.

I hummed in response and turned around to face him, giving him a kiss. But Daniel pulled away before things could get too heated. He sighed. "Work."

"Work," I agreed, just as unenthusiastic about the prospect. I felt foolish now for wasting the weekend when we could have been spending time together, wrapped up in bed for lazy hours between the sheets, or else curled up together on the couch, talking about anything and everything.

But there would be more weekends in our future, I was sure.

"Can I shower?" I asked Daniel.

"Only if I can join you," he said, his eyes gleaming wickedly.

"Work," I reminded him, but I grinned at the thought of showering together with him. I could already picture him in my mind's eye, the water running down his firm body, his hair slicked back and wet. I would be able to trail my fingers so easily down his body, tangling them in the soft, curly hairs at the base of his cock, the water easing my movements as I wrapped my fingers around him and pulled my grip along his length.

I blushed at the very thought of it. We had just had sex the night before, long and slow, and I had gotten off a couple of times. There was no reason why my body should already be this desperate for him, why my craving for him should already be this strong. With the way my body was reacting to the closeness of him, it felt as though we had gone weeks since the last time we had coupled.

But then again, I loved him. I guess maybe that was the difference between sex with him and sex with any other guy I had ever been with. The very thought of him could excite me.

I loved him.

We rolled out of bed, and Daniel chased me into the shower. He had his hands all over my body as we waited for the water to warm up. He kissed me until I was breathless, then moved me back beneath the spray. He continued to touch me, though, soaping up his hands and rubbing them along my skin, taking care not to miss a single spot.

I shivered, leaning into his ministrations, even though I knew that it couldn't go any further than this, these simple touches. We had to get to work. We had a lot to get done that day, even if I hadn't needed the extra time to catch Daniel up on everything that had happened at the end of the previous week. But it was nice, his naked appreciation of my body.

It didn't stop once we were cleaned up either. He held out a towel for me as I stepped out of the shower, and he rubbed me down with the soft material, using just the right amount of pressure to dry me off without rubbing too hard. "Why don't I get coffee and breakfast started while you get dressed and do your hair and makeup?" he suggested, hugging me close for one more moment.

"Sounds like a plan," I said, but I couldn't keep the wistfulness out of my voice. Another day.

Daniel smiled at me. "The trouble with dating the one person who can take my place while I'm gone is that there's really no way for both of us to play hooky without massively screwing up the schedule for later in the week," he lamented.

I laughed and gave him a nudge toward the door. "Get out of here before I drag you back to bed, then," I told him.

"Isn't that supposed to be my line?" he joked.

We headed into work like we had been every day prior to the trial: together, in Daniel's car, holding hands as we walked into the building. The press were out in droves that day, but it didn't sound like they had caught wind of anything that Duncan might have told them. Instead, the bulk of the attention seemed to be on Daniel. Everyone wanted to know more about the trial, as though they hadn't already grilled him on his way out of the courthouse on Friday.

Daniel answered a couple of questions good-naturedly and then led me forward with a hand at my lower back so that we could get in the building and get to work. He greeted a few people around the office as we entered, people he hadn't seen since before the trial. Everyone wanted to congratulate him on getting out relatively unscathed.

"So did you want to talk to me first about Thursday and Friday, or did you want to talk to Erin about the Duncan thing?" I asked in an undertone as we neared Daniel's office.

"I want to talk to Erin, but I want you to be there," Daniel said, smiling over at me. "You're my advisor, after all. I want to hear your read on the situation."

"You've already heard my read on the situation," I pointed out. "I let the guy go." I couldn't help sounding defensive about it.

But Daniel shook his head. "I'm not questioning what you did," he assured me, his hand at my lower back again for one brief moment. It was the most we'd touched in the office, and I noticed a couple of grins out the corner of my eye. But I forced my attention to remain focused on Daniel.

He lowered his voice even further. "I know the guys around the office trust me. But in light of what Duncan was asking about, I think it might be for the best if I'm not alone in my office with any of the women I work with if I can help it. Other than you, of course. Let them think what they will about that."

I snorted and shook my head. "If you keep the door open, though, surely no one will question that," I said.

Daniel shook his head as well. "I wish I could believe that. But the number of absurd things that the media has said about me at various points makes me a little worried," he admitted.

"That's fair," I said, nodding. I hadn't thought about things that way.

We headed into his office, and Erin followed after us at a word from Daniel. Daniel looked around with a grimace on his face. "I am so sorry I put you through all of this," he said to me, gesturing around at the mountains of paper.

I exchanged a look with Erin, and we both giggled while Daniel laughed. "All right, have a seat," he said to both of us. "Erin, I've heard something about Friday's incident, but I was hoping you could tell me exactly what Duncan said to you."

Erin nodded and outlined the situation again. I could feel my face flushed; I was still so embarrassed that I had let things happen the way they had. But I clung to the fact that Daniel said he would have done things exactly the same way if he had been the one in charge that day. I couldn't let it bother me.

Daniel nodded when Erin was finished, and I could tell that he was thinking long and hard about the situation. Finally, he shook his head, a grimace on his face. "I really wish there was more that we could do. But I'm afraid that Abby is probably right that it's all press we don't want at the moment.

"That's what we all think," Erin confirmed, nodding at Daniel. She shrugged, a grin on her face. "Anyway, it's not like he got anything damning out of any of us. We've never slept with you. Not much of a story there, unless he chooses to lie to the press about something. And if he does, then we can focus on a lawsuit to take him down over that. No harm, no foul."

Daniel nodded. He glanced over at me. "I also want to make sure we're scheduling time in Abby's and my schedule to get her more involved in the day-to-day CEO activities," he said. "I don't anticipate another lawsuit, but it bothers me that I didn't anticipate this one and ended up having to throw Abby into the thick of things like that. I should have been more prepared. If I don't want to bring in someone from outside the company to cover for me, then I need to make sure that I have a suitable stand-in here in the company."

"That makes sense," Erin said, nodding. I could see the corners of her mouth twitching into a grin. She glanced at her watch. "You could start by bringing her in to the meeting with Mr. Dorsey this morning. They haven't met yet. I don't think anyone in the company has met Dorsey except for you and I. But if she ever has to stand in for you, well. You know Dorsey."

Daniel rolled his eyes. "I know Dorsey," he agreed. "And that's a great idea. I forgot we had a meeting scheduled for this morning."

"Who's Mr. Dorsey?" I asked curiously.

"He's one of our biggest investors," Daniel explained.

"But he's a little bit intense," Erin whispered conspiratorially. "He basically doesn't acknowledge anyone around the office except for Daniel. Says he doesn't have time to be friendly with people."

"He's nice enough," Daniel interrupted quickly. "He's not going to be rude to you or anything. He's just, I guess, focused. Like what's happening in his brain is the most important thing in the world, to the exclusion of all else."

I snorted. I was a little worried to meet this man, but if Erin and Daniel both thought it was a good idea, I supposed I didn't really have much of a choice. Anyway, I wanted to be a CEO one day. That meant that I had to get used to interacting with different types of people. This was a great place to start.

"Don't be nervous," Daniel whispered in my ear a little while later as we headed to the conference room where Mr. Dorsey was waiting for us. He was pressed in close to me, his lips brushing the shell of my ear. And then he was gone again, opening the door and gesturing for me to enter before him.

I tripped over the threshold but managed to right myself before I toppled headlong into the room. Still, I was sure I was blushing as I held out a hand to Mr. Dorsey.

"Bode, this is my advisor, Abby James," Daniel said smoothly. I could see the hint of a grin on his face, but he kept his eyes on the investor. "I hope you don't mind that she'll be joining us for our meeting today?"

"No problem at all," Dorsey said, reaching out to shake my hand. But he was already turning back to Daniel. "So about those latest acquisitions."

They moved swiftly on to the business at hand, and I struggled to keep up. Daniel had briefed me on some of the business before we had come in to the meeting, but I still felt like I didn't quite know enough about the company to keep up.

Still, it was all interesting, and I made sure to jot down the questions I had for Daniel. I was sure I'd get a chance to ask all of them later. And despite the fact that on Friday I had felt sure that I would never actually be a CEO, that I wasn't even sure anymore that was something I might want, I now felt tons more confident than I had before.

Maybe it was just that I had Daniel by my side now. But I didn't think it was just that. It was more his easy confidence in me, the fact that he thought it was worth training me up. The fact that he had so easily brushed off my mistake from the previous week.

I smiled to myself as I continued to jot down notes. Maybe I could make it after all. I just had to believe in myself.

Same as for my relationship with Daniel. Maybe we could make everything okay. Make everything work out. We just had to believe in it.

Chapter 19

Daniel

AFTER LAST WEEK HAD been such a mess, I should have known that this week would feel ten thousand times better. Abby and I had shown up at work together every morning, and there had been no more uncomfortable media encounters for her. Not only that, but I had gotten to wake up next to her every day.

Things were going well around the office, too. I had helped her to pass off some of the normal advisor duties to one of the other guys who worked in the office, and she had extra time to shadow me and learn more about the company from a CEO perspective. She was coming along well in her training, and I had to admit, I was pretty damned proud of her for everything.

She was going to make an amazing CEO one day.

Of course, she thought I was just training her up in case I needed her to take over for me for a few days in the future. Or for when she was ready to leave McGregor Enterprises and go on to another company. That wasn't quite the case, but I wasn't ready to have a serious conversation with her yet about how if I had my way, she would work for my family's business for the rest of her life—right by my side.

I was selfish like that. I didn't want all her talent going off to one of my competitors.

There was a lot that we would need to talk about, but I didn't want to make her any more nervous than I had to. Because she was nervous, I could tell. I didn't know if it was because of her perceived mistake the previous week with Duncan or if she was just generally nervous about having all this responsibility one day, but I definitely noticed an uptick in her usual clumsiness. She would trip walking into the conference room or blurt out a question in the middle of a meeting and then slap a hand over her mouth. That kind of thing.

She always looked embarrassed when those things happened. Then, she would give me a sheepish look, one that made me sure she expected me to kick her out of the meeting or something.

But of course I wasn't going to do anything like that. In fact, every little clumsy mistake she made just made me think she was even more adorable.

"What are you thinking about?" Abby asked from across the table.

I shook my head, grinning at her. "You," I told her. "Have I mentioned that you look particularly beautiful tonight?"

Abby blushed and ducked her head. "You might have," she said, but I could tell that she was pleased with the praise. And I wasn't just saying it to be nice. I had asked her to come out to dinner with me and told her that I wanted to take her someplace fancy. But I still hadn't expected her to pull out the stops like she had.

She had left her blonde hair in loose waves that fell down around her shoulders, and she was wearing a stunning backless dress in lipstick red. I could just see a bit of a lacy black bra peeking out from the low-cut neckline, and I wanted nothing more than to drag her home with me.

It was definitely a change from the way she dressed around the office. And I would never ask her to dress like this all the time. I liked her relaxed look around the house, and I liked the professional look she had at work. But this—I definitely wasn't complaining about the way she looked tonight. If it hadn't been as fancy a place as it was, I might have dragged her off to the bathrooms to have my way with her there.

Of course, if it hadn't been as fancy a place as it was, she probably wouldn't be dressed like that.

I watched Abby shiver a little, and I frowned. "Are you cold?" I asked.

"No," Abby said, shaking her head. "It's just that the way that you're looking at me..." She leaned forward, lowering her voice. "I think we can do without dessert. I'm not going to last much longer with you looking at me like that."

I laughed. "I was thinking exactly the same thing," I told her.

We finished up our dinner, chatting easily about the things we could do together that weekend. I didn't care what we did as long as I got to spend time with her. I still couldn't help thinking back to the previous weekend, when she'd been ignoring my calls. I definitely didn't want to go back to that. Anything else would be preferable.

"Sir, I just wanted to let you know that there are a number of photographers out front," the maître d' informed me in an undertone as we were putting on our coats. "Our guys are, of course, doing their best to manage the situation, but it might be advisable for you and your lovely dining companion to leave through the back."

I glanced over at Abby, who was smiling at us. She shook her head slightly. "It's all right," she said. "Let's give them a few photos. Maybe it'll help cover up all the bad press from last week."

"Are you sure?" I asked, remembering what she had originally said about wanting to stay out of the media's eye. For a second, my mind flashed back to Ivy. But that was ridiculous. There had never been a time when Ivy didn't want to be in full view of the media. And besides, what Abby said about covering up the stories from the trial made sense.

Because there had been plenty of stories all week. I hadn't really read through any of them, not even the ones that Austin had forwarded over to me. For some reason, that week it had been easier to just ignore all of them. I could imagine, by now, the kinds of things they might be saying about me. And I realized I just didn't care.

If people wanted to believe the media about me, so be it. The people that I worked with knew the real side of me. People like Abby would never believe the shit that was there in the tabloids about me. I just needed to surround myself with more people who didn't care about all of that garbage. Keep reminding myself that if people didn't want to do business with me over all of that, they probably weren't the kinds of people that I wanted to do business with anyway.

Abby smiled at me. "Look, I've been thinking about this. And it's up to you—if you want to sneak out the back then we will. I just think that if we control more of our narrative, give them a few good images of us together and give them tame stories about the two of us, it'll keep them happy without them going wild speculating on all sorts of crazy things. They'll have their column about our date night, rather than making up some stupid shit about how we do business together."

"That's a good point," I said, nodding at her. "If we show them that we have nothing to hide, they'll realize that we have nothing to hide." I grinned. "Although I do like the idea of running out the back with you. It seems more exciting."

Abby snorted and gestured down at her outfit, including her heels. "I'm not fit to be running anywhere tonight," she pointed out. Then, she winked at me. "But I'm pretty sure I make suitable arm candy for the hottest young billionaire in Chicago?"

I laughed and pulled her into my arms for a moment, kissing her. "You always make suitable arm candy, as far as I'm concerned," I promised her. I pulled away, and she finished buttoning up her jacket.

"All right, let's go," she said.

There weren't as many photographers out front as I had expected, although we were both nearly blinded by flashbulbs the second we walked out together. I looped an arm around Abby, pulling her close and steadying her in case she had any of those clumsy jitters I had seen around the office. I tried to smile rather than grimace at the blinding lights. It was easier when I glanced down at Abby at the same time that she smiled dazzlingly up at me.

"They've got their photos—now take me home," she demanded in an undertone, startling a laugh out of me.

We headed over to my car, where the driver was waiting. Together, one after the other, we slipped into the back seat. Abby giggled as we pulled away. "So that's what it's like to feel like a movie star, I guess," she said.

I shook my head, making a face. "Sorry about that. Again," I said.

Abby shrugged. "It wasn't your fault," she pointed out. "And anyway, it was my suggestion that we actually let them take some photos."

"A brilliant suggestion, too," I told her, brushing back a lock of her hair. "Yet another example of what a great CEO you'll make one day."

Abby blushed and ducked her head. "That's a long way off," she said.

I leaned in and kissed her, and she moved eagerly against me. As we kissed, I couldn't keep myself from unbuttoning her jacket, my fingers tracing the low-cut neckline, touching the edges of her breasts, that teasing bit of lace I'd caught flashes of all evening.

"You drive me wild," I told her between kisses.

Abby smirked at me, reaching down to fondle me in my slacks. "I'd noticed," she said, and I groaned.

"You don't know how many unsexy things I had to think just so that I could stand up and walk out of there without embarrassing myself," I admitted, and she laughed.

"There are definitely times when I'm glad I'm not a dude," she said.

"I am *very* glad you're not," I joked, pulling her in for another heated kiss, my hand making its way up her inner thigh so that she squirmed against me. "Number one reason to hire a driver." I laughed as Abby straddled my lap suddenly, grinding down against me.

She giggled but didn't stop moving against me, her panties dragging along the tip of my still-clothed erection. I growled and looped a hand around the back of her neck, pulling her down toward me so we could continue sloppily making out. I barely noticed when we reached my house.

Finally, I released her. "Inside. Now," I panted. Abby wasted no time in scrambling out of the car and waiting for me to lead the way.

I grabbed her the second we were in the foyer with the door shut behind us. I pinned her back against the wall, my fingers back between her legs, pushing her panties out of the way so that I could finger her open. There was no way I could make it upstairs with her right now. I felt like my whole body would combust if I didn't get inside of her right now. And from the breathy moans that she was making, I was sure she was in complete agreement.

I unbuckled my slacks, freeing my prick from its confinement at long last, gasping when Abby reached down a hand between us so that she could tug me to full hardness. I scooped her up into my arms, pressing her back against the wall, and thrust into her.

Chapter 20

Abby

I GASPED AS DANIEL lifted me into his arms right there in the hall, driving his hard cock into my slick entrance. It was what the whole night had been working toward, really. When Daniel had suggested on Wednesday afternoon that we should go out for a fancy dinner on Friday evening to celebrate the end of the trial and the start of my good training toward one day becoming a CEO, I had hatched the plan to dress as nicely as I could.

I had enlisted Leanne's help to find the perfect dress on Thursday evening after work. Her jaw had dropped when I'd walked out in this red number, and I knew that it was the perfect choice.

I'd actually been a little nervous putting it on for Daniel on Friday evening, though. Would he think that it was too slutty? Was I sending the wrong message? I knew that he was looking for someone who was smart, someone who wasn't just another airheaded bimbo. But then again, he had seen me in my office clothes nearly every day since I had started working at McGregor Enterprises. He had seen me in jeans around the house. He had seen me in nicer dresses.

And he knew what he was getting into with me. I couldn't possibly think I was sending the wrong message to him. Sometimes, I was sure that he knew me better than I even knew myself.

Now, as he rocked into me, I didn't regret my choice of outfit at all. No, I had made the right choice. I had gotten him at least as turned on as he had gotten me. I didn't know why I was so turned on by his presence across the table from me at dinner. He was just in another of his suits, this one definitely nice but not markedly different from what he wore around the office during the day. But he kept reaching across the table to touch my hand, laughing at the things I said about the challenges of work that week, and just making me feel so comfortable around him.

I loved him. That was all I could think about as I grinned stupidly over at him. And the thing was, I could tell he was thinking the same thing.

We were still on the same page at the moment, as he pressed me against the wall. I clung to his shoulders, using them to move my body as well, heat coiling in my belly as he continued to work my body in the way that only he seemed able to do.

I couldn't get over how strong he was, or the fact that he was so effortlessly able to move my body like this, holding me up as though I was light as a feather. I could feel his muscles beneath the material of his jacket as I clung to him. I could barely believe we were like this, unable to keep our hands off each other, unable to make it past the foyer or out of our clothing before we fucked each other breathless.

It was exciting, it was wonderful, it was everything I could ever have wanted.

I gasped, pushing my palms back against the wall as my back arched. A tingle ran down my spine as he managed to hit that one incredible bundle of nerves inside of me, the one that made my blood sing. Between that and the way my panties were still pressed against my clit, giving me the perfect kind of friction as Daniel continued to rock into me, I was so close to the edge already, or maybe I had been for the entire night.

I sobbed as I came, but Daniel wasn't done with me yet. He pulled me closer to him, carrying me toward the kitchen as I continued to gasp for air, not pulling out, his cock still twitching with impatience inside of me. He set me down on one of the high barstools and continued to slam into me with wild abandon as I held on for dear life.

I couldn't tell if the waves of pleasure overwhelming me would ever end. It certainly felt like they wouldn't. Each new thrust sent another pulse of heat through me, until my whole body felt raw with feeling, a pulsing livewire, all circuits shorted out with the amazing feeling of it all.

Daniel finally groaned, spilling inside of me, steadying himself against the countertop behind me, his face pressed sideways against my breast. "Fuck," he said as he finally slumped toward me.

I laughed, giddy with the epic release. "You can say that again." I sighed and shook my head, plucking at my dress, suddenly aware of the fact that I was still wearing it. And suddenly aware of just how much I wanted to go upstairs and tumble naked into bed with him, our normal routine. "So I take it you like the dress?"

Daniel laughed and shook his head, leaning in to kiss me chastely. "You look amazing," he told me. He ran his fingers back through his mussed hair. "But now I'm exhausted."

"Me too," I admitted. "Bed?"

Daniel nodded, scooping me back into his arms and carrying me up the stairs as I giggled.

"So I did promise that when the trial was all done, I would take you somewhere where we could be alone," he reminded me quietly as we lay there naked in the dark together.

I blinked and rolled around toward him, looking up at his face in the half-light of moonlight spilling in through the window. "I thought now that I'm your replacement around the office, though, we couldn't both play hooky."

Daniel shrugged. "I wasn't suggesting we play hooky," he said, grinning at me. "I was suggesting that we both clear our schedules in the near future. Where do you want to go?"

I bit my lower lip. "I don't even know," I lied. Where did I want to go to be alone with Daniel? Was he really suggesting that we take a trip together, or was he just teasing me?

"Sure you do," Daniel said encouragingly. "Come on, where do you want to go? We can go anywhere in the world."

"I've always wanted to go to Thailand," I admitted shyly. I could picture us there on an island, with a cute little secluded bungalow just for the two of us. We could spend the days curled together, exploring each other's bodies, all worries about work fading far away.

"Thailand," Daniel said, and I could hear the interested note in his voice, like he was really considering it. I suddenly realized that I didn't even know if he was a beach person or not. Maybe he hated the humidity, and here I was, suggesting that we go to one of the warmest, most humid places on the planet.

"Or Australia," I added, figuring that would give him another option. "That's another place I've always thought about going. I mean, to be honest, there are so many places I'd like to go."

"But those are the top two," Daniel said. He shrugged. "Well, why don't we do both of them? Money's not an object. And I want to show you the world."

I giggled and curled my body closer to his. "Are you serious?" I asked him.

"One hundred percent," Daniel said, nodding at me. He kissed my forehead. "I'll start making the plans." Then, softly: "I love you, you know."

"I love you, too." I sighed happily. I drifted off to a sleep filled with dreams of bungalows, elephants, and hill treks. All with Daniel by my side.

Chapter 21

Daniel

I ASKED ERIN TO COME into my office while Abby was at lunch. She gave me a curious look as she came in. "What's going on?" she asked.

"I want to rearrange my schedule some," I said.

"Okay," Erin said, her brow furrowing. "What kind of rearranging are we talking about here? You're not getting enough time to show Abby the ropes with that new CEO training that you're working on?"

"Not exactly," I said, shaking my head. "I promised Abby that when the whole trial thing was over, I would take her away somewhere with me. You know, as thanks for letting me throw her to the wolves as interim CEO and all."

Erin rolled her eyes, smirking at me. "I'm sure that's the only reason you want to whisk her away," she teased.

I grinned at her and shrugged. "I have to admit, I'm excited to just take a little break and get to spend some quality time with her," I said. "But the main thing is, if I'm gone and she's gone, even if I bring in someone to oversee things in our absence, there's not a lot of business meetings and things that can happen without either of us."

Erin nodded slowly. "So basically we need to try to block off, what? A week? Two weeks?"

"As long as you can give me," I told her. "I know it's probably irresponsible to ask for that, but I'm just hoping to take her to as many beautiful places as I can. She suggested Thailand and Australia; the transit alone, plus the time changes, are already going to eat part of that time."

"Of course," Erin said. She scrolled through the calendar on her tablet, muttering to herself for a moment. "Yeah, we can do this," she said finally. "Push back some of the important meetings. People will understand. And they'll wait to do business with you. McGregor Enterprises has a reputation; everyone knows you're the best." She grinned at me, and I grinned right back.

"I'll get on it this afternoon and let you know what I come up with," she told me finally.

"Sounds perfect," I said. "And if there's anyone pushing back against their meetings being rescheduled, feel free to transfer them over to me so that I can subtly remind them that I've chained myself to this desk for the better part of the last decade."

Erin snorted with amusement. But then, she frowned across at me. "The only thing I want to ask is, have you thought about how the media might try to spin this one? You've just gotten out of the trial with Gerrard, and now it looks like you're trying to lay low for a while or something."

I shrugged. "To be honest, I don't give a damn what the media has to say on the matter," I told her, and for the first time in my life, it was true. It was the same thing I'd been thinking before: the people I actually cared about weren't about to mistake the sensationalized tabloid stories for the truth about my life. And the people who did believe all the nonsense the media said about me I didn't care to have in my life anymore. I wanted more Abbys and less Ivys.

Erin looked pleased by my response. "All right, then," she said. "If you give me a list of places you're trying to visit, I can look into booking the accommodations and flights and everything as well."

I shook my head. "Actually, I think this time, Abby and I are going to do all of that ourselves. And I don't think we'll plan the whole trip ahead of time. I want things to be flexible when we hit the ground. I don't want to miss out on anything we want to do."

"You mean, you don't want her to miss out on anything she wants to do," Erin surmised with a knowing smile on her face.

"Exactly," I said.

"Sounds good," Erin said. She paused. "You really care about her, don't you?" she asked softly.

I nodded. "I really do," I admitted. It was strange admitting that to someone around the office, but I knew I could trust Erin. Besides, no one around the office really seemed to mind that Abby and I were a thing. In fact, I was pretty sure people were mostly relieved that I wasn't alone anymore. I had always tried to maintain a more relaxed environment around the office, but now it was starting to feel even more relaxed, and efficient, than normal. I chalked that up to Abby's presence in my life.

"And the overseer for while you're gone?" Erin asked. "Any idea who that might be? Is that friend of yours still between projects?"

"He might be," I said. "But I've decided that it's really important for me not to hire in someone from the outside. I want someone who really understands this company's heart and soul. Someone who everyone around the office can respect."

"Oh," Erin said, looking puzzled. "But if you're gone and Abby's gone, who did you have in mind?" I could see her wracking her brains and knew that she probably expected I'd hire one of the guys who had once worked for my father.

But instead, I smiled at her. "Actually, Erin, I was wondering if you'd be willing to step up while I'm out."

Erin looked shocked. "Me?" she squeaked in surprise. "But I'm just your assistant. I'm about as far removed from CEO as it's possible to get and still be in the same building."

"Not really, when you think about it," I said, shaking my head. "There was a reason I asked you to help Abby while I was gone. You're smart. And because you're my assistant, you know more about this business than most people do. You've scheduled meetings with everyone I work with, and you know what any given team is working on at any given time."

"I guess so," Erin said doubtfully.

"Besides, I'm not asking you to step up and be a CEO while we're gone," I assured Erin. "Not that I think that you couldn't handle it, but I know it wouldn't be fair for me to put that pressure on you. Really, I'm just looking for you to keep things running smoothly. To handle whatever anyone throws at the business while we're gone, and to keep me in the loop about things that you think I need to know about. I trust you to know which things are important and which ones can wait until we're back."

Erin nodded slowly. "I guess so," she said.

"And I'm not asking you to be perfect either," I added. "Just like I wasn't asking for Abby to be perfect when she stepped up for me. Things like the Duncan situation, those may happen. They could happen even if I was here, because fuck knows that I'm not perfect either. In fact, you should talk to some of the older guys sometime about all the mistakes I made when I first took over for my father." I shook my head. "I'm really just asking you to keep the wheels turning. I know it's a lot, but I wouldn't be asking if I didn't believe you could do this."

Erin smiled tentatively at me. "All right," she finally said. "But on one condition."

"What's that?" I asked, expecting that she would ask for a raise. One which I would gladly give her. In fact, I had already drawn up the paperwork to send over to HR as early as that afternoon if she agreed to handle things while I was gone. To be honest, she deserved it for everything she did for me.

But she didn't ask for a raise. Instead, she gave me a cheeky grin. "Just promise me you're not going to leave me as many notes as you left for Abby," she said. "Or I swear, I'm going to run screaming for the hills."

I snorted but nodded at her. "It's a deal," I told her. "But seriously, you don't have to agree to all of this right now. We don't even know when we'll be able to go just yet. If you want more time to think it over, that's all right."

Erin shook her head as she got to her feet. "Nah," she said. "I'll do it. After everything you and Abby have been through with the press and this trial and everything else, you deserve some time away, just the two of you. Especially since dragging you away from this office is usually a chore in and of itself. I'm glad you've found someone who can get you to even think about taking a holiday."

I snorted and rolled my eyes, but Erin was smirking teasingly at me again. "Yeah, yeah, get out of here," I said, flapping my hands at her. But when she was almost to the door, I added, "Thanks, Erin."

"Don't mention it, boss," she said, flashing a grin over her shoulder at me. She left, shutting the door behind her, and I let out a breath I hadn't even realized I was holding.

Chapter 22

Abby

I WALKED INTO THE BAR on Tuesday night and smiled when I saw that Leanne was already there, sitting by herself in a booth in the back and sipping at her drink while she scrolled through something on her phone. I dropped into the seat across from her. "Hey, you," I said to her. It was so rare that we got these girls' nights like this, and I didn't want to waste a moment of it.

Leanne grinned over at me. "Hey, yourself," she said. "You're late."

"I know, I know." I sighed, holding up my hands apologetically. "Daniel and I were working on a game plan for the meeting we have tomorrow, and the next thing I knew, it was past time for me to leave."

"Oh really?" Leanne asked, raising an eyebrow at me, and I could tell from the way she was smirking that she didn't believe me for a moment.

I snorted and shook my head. "It's not like that," I told her. "We're strictly hands off from one another while we're at the office. Even in private."

"Even after everyone else has gone home?" Leanne asked. "Where's the fun in that?"

I shrugged. "Easier to draw the lines and stick to them," I pointed out. "Besides, you know how the media would be if they even so much as heard from someone who heard from someone that Daniel and I were behaving inappropriately around the office. They'd have a field day."

Leanne sighed. "Yeah. And the columns about your suitability as Daniel's advisor have only just finally started being nice."

"To be honest, I haven't been reading them," I admitted. "I know that's probably bad, that I should keep on top of at least everything they're saying about me. There's no way of knowing how that could all affect my future, after all. But I just can't find it in me to care about it. At the moment, I'm happy with where I am, so there's no point in worrying how it'll affect my future job searches."

"Fair enough," Leanne said. "I think that's a good way to look at things. And I'd let you know if there was anything in there that you really needed to know about."

"I know you would," I said, smiling at her.

"What are best friends for?" Leanne joked. "So things are going well around the office, though? Daniel isn't overworking you, is he?"

I shrugged again. "To be honest, he tries to get me to go home earlier than him most times. But I don't want him to be the last person in the office every night. I think he gets that now, so he's actually started to leave a bit earlier, too. It's probably better for both of us that way."

"Definitely sounds like it," Leanne said, nodding. "And as long as you like the work, I guess it's not such a bad thing. Just make sure you take some time for fun as well."

"We do," I told her, smiling. To be honest, things with Daniel were so much fun. More so than I could ever have imagined. We could spend hours together just doing nothing, just chatting, and it never got old. I wanted to tell her all about the trip that Daniel had hinted at, but I wanted to wait until I had more solid information about it first.

It wasn't that I didn't believe Daniel when he said that he wanted to take me away somewhere with him, that he wanted to show me the world. But I knew that arranging time off for the both of us would be problematic logistically, and I didn't want to get my hopes up in case he determined that it was impossible for us. I knew just how important his business was for him, and I didn't want to put any sort of pressure on him.

"So what's new with you?" I asked Leanne to change the subject slightly.

Leanne shrugged, taking another sip of her drink. "Well, actually, Matt and I are thinking about trying for another baby," she said casually.

I gaped at her. "Leanne!" I exclaimed. "That's amazing. Any luck yet?"

Leanne shook her head. "We're still mostly just thinking about it," she admitted. "But I'm pretty sure we're going to go for it. We both always thought that three was the perfect number. And now that Layla is old enough that we don't have to worry about her so much, I guess it just seems like the perfect time to have another one." She wrinkled her nose. "Of course, I've finally given away all the baby things and gotten used to not having to change diapers anymore."

I laughed and shook my head as well. "You know that as soon as you have a new bundle of joy, you'll forget all about the bad parts," I reminded her. "Or at least, if you don't forget about them, you'll realize that it's all worth it in the end."

Leanne smiled. "That, I know," she said. "It's all worth it in the end."

"I mean, you already have two perfect little angels," I added. "You seem to know what you're doing, at least."

Leanne snorted. "To be honest, I don't think you ever really feel like you know what you're doing as a parent. But somehow, everything seems to work itself out. Or at least, that's my experience with it."

I giggled. "Well, I look forward to having a new little niece or nephew, if you do decide to go for it," I told her.

"You look forward to spoiling the little one!" Leanne joked, and I had to laugh. "And what about you?" she asked. "Do you think you'll ever give me a little niece or nephew to spoil?"

I sighed and shook my head. "I don't know, Leanne."

Leanne raised an eyebrow at me. "You don't know?" she echoed. "That's at least a change from the straight up 'no' you always said before."

I smiled at her. "It is a change," I allowed. "And I don't know if I'll ever actually go through with it. But that night that Daniel and you guys and the kids and I all had dinner together, I was just watching him there at the table with them, imagining what it would be like if he and I had a family to have family dinners with. I don't know."

Leanne smiled. "That's how it starts," she warned me. We both laughed. "And what about Daniel?" she asked. "Have you talked to him about it? Having kids?"

I shook my head. "Not yet," I admitted. "As you know, things haven't been easy between the two of us. There's been a lot of drama. I didn't want to rush things."

"These are conversations that you guys need to have," Leanne reminded me.

"I know," I said. "I just don't want to scare him off or anything."

"Do you really think you would?" Leanne asked exasperatedly. "You've seen him with Zach and Layla. The guy is wonderful with them. And you know I don't say that about a lot of people."

I laughed. "I know," I said again. I sighed. "I guess what I'm really worried about is just getting in over my head. Even further than I already am. You know, I really like this guy. Love him, even. And he said that he loves me, too, but all the same, I'm just worried."

"Wait, back up a minute," Leanne said, holding up both hands. "He said he loves you?"

I blushed and nodded. "Yeah," I admitted. "It was the night he came over to your guys' place. When he and I had been fighting. He told me he never should have treated a woman he loves the way he treated me."

"Aww, that's so cute," Leanne said, smiling at me. "So if he loves you, why are you so worried? At least it sounds like the two of you are on the same page, even if you haven't been dating so long. Or are you still afraid that things with the media could get difficult?"

"It's not that," I said, shaking my head. "And I know that this isn't fair to him. But I'm just worried that one day either Daniel is going to do something that makes me realize he really has been an ass all along, or else he's going to get sick of me or something. You know I don't have the greatest track record with guys."

It sounded so self-deprecating just to say it out loud like that. It wasn't like I had self-esteem issues, not really. But I really was worried that somehow, things with Daniel and I were going to fizzle out eventually. I didn't want to get too attached to him if that was the case.

"It's just, every time that I start making plans for the future, I check myself," I explained to Leanne before she could say anything. "Because I know that that's the worst part of any breakup: having those plans for the future that you made with the other person and realizing that none of those things are actually going to happen now, or that you can never do certain things again without thinking about them."

Leanne winced. "There's a lot to unpack there," she said.

"I know." I sighed. "And like I said, I know none of that is fair to Daniel."

"Yeah, but you have to be fair to yourself. I get that," Leanne said, nodding at me. She reached out and caught my hands where they rested against the worn, wooden table. "I know that you haven't had the best track record with guys," she said slowly. "But you also know that Matt and I weren't stoked about you being with Daniel originally, and we've come around. You don't think we would have done that if we thought the guy was an asshole, do you?"

I laughed. "No, I guess not," I admitted. "But still, something could happen."

"It could," Leanne agreed, nodding. "Tomorrow, you could be hit by a bus on your way to work, rendering all plans for the future as meaningless. Maybe you'd never become a CEO, even. But does that mean you should stop your training with Daniel to one day lead a company?"

"No," I said immediately, shaking my head. I frowned. "You know, when you put it that way, it sounds really silly," I admitted.

"It's not that it's silly," Leanne said. "I get why you're nervous. Hell, you know how nervous I was when I first started dating your brother. Not least of which because I was afraid that if he and I ever broke up, you would be obligated to take his side. I didn't want to lose my best friend as well as the guy I was crushing on."

I grinned. "At least I don't have to worry about that," I agreed.

Leanne shrugged. "Just, I think that if things feel this right with Daniel, if you're willing to forget about all the drama with the media and everything else, then maybe it's worth making some long-term plans with him."

"You're right," I agreed. I sighed. "The thing about it is, though, there's so many things that I want in a future with him."

"Such as?" Leanne asked.

"Kids," I admitted. "I want to get married and move in together and have kids. I want to travel with him, and not just for work. You know that I've always wanted to be a CEO one day, but for Daniel, I don't know. I either want to be a fantastic CEO at a company that really makes a difference, or..." I trailed off, feeling silly.

"Or?" Leanne prodded.

"Or maybe I'd be ready to give up the idea of being a CEO if it meant that I could keep working with Daniel as his advisor," I admitted. I groaned and put my head in my hands as I heard the words leave my mouth. "And I know that it's way too soon to be thinking along those lines, but there it is. That's all I've been able to think about since he started training me more in what is necessary to be a CEO. I'm not sure that I ever want to leave McGregor Enterprises."

"Honestly, that's kind of refreshing to hear, with the way that you've bounced through jobs since your graduation," Leanne teased.

I had to laugh at that. But then, I shook my head. "It's just, I've always wanted to be a CEO," I reminded her. "I feel like I shouldn't be basing my future so totally on Daniel that I'm willing to give up everything I've always wanted, just to be with him."

"You're not," Leanne protested. "If you think that you want to keep working alongside him, then you're not giving up everything that you've always wanted. And not only that, but forget all about that nonsense about it being too soon to be making those sorts of plans. If things are right, then things are right."

"I guess so," I said, frowning as I thought it over.

"Besides," Leanne added, a twinkle in her eyes, "if you're going to have kids, someone is going to need to look after them. Maybe it's a good thing if the two of you can split the role of CEO so that there's always someone home with the kids."

I grinned at her. "The kids?" I asked jokingly. "How many are we having, then?"

"I guess we'll have to see," Leanne said, smiling at me. "You know, I'm really happy for you. I'm glad that you found someone you like finally. And a good one, too."

"We're not getting married yet," I reminded her, caution in my tone.

But Leanne just rolled her eyes. "Oh, I know," she said. "I'm sure I'll be the first person you tell when you are getting married. But anyway, what I'm saying is that it doesn't hurt to plan things. Matt and I talked about kids and everything else when we'd only been dating for, like, a month. And sure, we had known each other for longer than that since we all basically grew up together starting in high school. But all the same."

"I'll think about talking to him about some of it," I promised Leanne. "I'm not saying we'll make any firm plans just yet, but I guess if things are going to go anywhere at all, then we kind of need a road map."

"Exactly," Leanne said. "And hey, why don't the two of you come over for family dinner again this coming Sunday? If he's going to be a staple in your life, Matt and I want to get to know him better. And like I said, he's great with the kids."

"Sounds like a plan," I said, smiling.

Chapter 23

Daniel

I HEARD ABBY'S CAR pull up outside on Tuesday evening and smiled to myself. She had gone for drinks with Leanne that night, a much-needed girls' night she had told me. I knew that she hadn't had a chance to see just Leanne, without the kids or Matt being there, in a while now. So as much as I would have liked to have her all to myself for the evening, I was glad she had gone. But I was equally glad that she was back relatively early, I had to admit.

I liked having her around the mansion with me. Somehow, she filled all those empty spaces that had bothered me ever since Austin had moved out. Somehow, even when we weren't talking, when we were just curled up together reading or working in the living room, Abby seemed to kill those terrible silences.

But I had used her absence that night to work on something slightly different, and I was proud of myself for getting everything done before Abby came inside.

She paused when she found me in the living room. "Hey," she said, smiling at me. "What's that look for?"

"I have something for you," I told her slowly, and I watched the excited curiosity fill her eyes.

"Oh really?" she asked, coming over to the couch and sitting down next to me. She leaned in for a quick kiss. "What is it?" she asked.

I reached over to the coffee table and grabbed the white envelope I had placed there. "Now, I know that me handing you envelopes has a little history to it. Something that we'd rather not repeat," I said slowly, and Abby laughed. "This is a good surprise, I promise you," I told her.

Abby flipped over the envelope and lifted the flap, pulling out the papers from inside. Her jaw dropped. "Is this for real?" she asked.

"One hundred percent," I promised her, grinning at her hushed excitement. "Two one-way tickets to Thailand, one for me and one for you, leaving in a little over two weeks." I paused. "I moved around some of our meetings, with Erin's help. I have to admit, I was kind of surprised to find out how willing everyone was to let me take a vacation. I guess a lifetime of great service pays off eventually."

Abby shook her head, still looking stunned. "And the other employees?" she asked. "What did they say?"

"I haven't told everyone yet," I admitted. "But I think things are going to be fine. They'll be in Erin's capable hands."

Abby's head snapped up. "You're putting her in charge as interim CEO?" she asked, and I couldn't read the expression on her face. Having recently put Abby in that position, though, and realizing just how uncomfortable it had made her, I could imagine some of what she was thinking, though. Hell, she was probably wondering what would happen if Erin outshone her. If I would keep Erin as my advisor instead or something.

"I didn't ask her to be interim CEO, no," I said quickly, keeping my voice gentle. "She'll basically be doing the same thing that she's always done, only with a bit more scope now. She'll be in charge of making things run as smoothly as possible in our absence and letting us know about everything that we need to handle right away. The meetings that can't be rescheduled, she'll sit in on them and take detailed notes for us. That sort of thing."

"Oh wow," Abby said, shaking her head. "And you really think this will work?"

I shook my head as well. "To be honest, Abby, I don't really care if it works or not. All I know is that as irresponsible as it may sound, all I want to do is show you all the places you've always dreamed of seeing."

A slow grin broke across Abby's face. "Thank you," she said quietly.

"Thank *you*," I said to her in response. "You know, before you came along, the only thing I could focus on was work. And I definitely love my company and the work we do. This isn't the end of that. But on the other hand, you've made me want so much more than just that."

"How long are we going for?" Abby asked, looking down at the tickets again. "These are just one-ways."

"I know," I said. "There are two reasons for that. The first is that if anything big does happen with the company and I need to fly back right away, or we both need to fly back right away, we have the flexibility to do so. Of course, I'm hoping that nothing like that happens, but I figured we should be on the safe side either way. We can always pick back up once everything settles down again, so don't worry about that."

"Makes sense," Abby said.

"The other reason is that this leaves us free to pick our own route once we're over there," I continued. "Rather than lock ourselves into a certain amount of time in Thailand followed by a certain amount of time in Australia, this gives us the chance to explore for as long as we want. Maybe we only end up seeing Thailand. Or maybe on the way down to Australia, we decide to stop off in Indonesia or somewhere as well. I just didn't think it made sense to lock ourselves into anything."

"I love that plan," Abby said, grinning at me. She shook her head, though. "I still can't believe this is real," she said. "I feel like you need to pinch me or something."

I laughed and gave her a hug. "How was drinks with Leanne anyway?" I asked.

Abby seemed at a loss for words for a moment. Then, she smiled. "Not nearly as exciting as this," she joked. But her eyes turned serious again. "Really, Daniel. I can't imagine a better gift than this. Getting to see the world with you? That's amazing." She paused. "Thanks again."

I leaned down to press a soft kiss against her lips. "Thank *you* again," I murmured. "I know you don't believe I was ever the terrible person that the tabloids make me out to be, but still, I have to thank you for always believing in me."

Abby grinned up at me as we pulled apart, then got to her feet, setting aside the envelope and pulling me up to my feet as well. "Let's go upstairs," she suggested. "I think this time, it's my turn to show you how truly grateful I am."

Chapter 24

Abby

I ROLLED OFF OF DANIEL and flopped down against the mattress, just trying to catch my breath. Daniel twisted his fingers in mine, but it was clear that all he could do was breathe for the moment, too. No matter how many times we'd had sex this week, it seemed like we kept reaching higher and higher degrees of ecstasy. Each time I came, I was sure that I could never cum so hard again. But each time we made love, Daniel seemed intent on proving me wrong.

I certainly wasn't complaining.

But now, as I looked at the time, I groaned. "Maybe I should just call Leanne and tell her that we can't make it to dinner tonight," I said to Daniel. "Some work emergency."

Daniel grinned at me, rolling toward me and propping himself up on one arm. With his other hand, he traced the curve of my breast, making me shiver as lust flared anew in the pit of my belly. "Or maybe we both have some terrible disease that makes us unable to make it out of bed," he agreed gravely.

I giggled and pushed his hand away, sighing. "We should probably get going," I said.

"I thought you were almost ready anyway," Daniel reminded me.

I snorted. "That was before you tore off my dress and tangled your fingers through my hair," I pointed out. "If I don't want to look like I was just fucked, and I don't since we're going to Leanne and Matt's place and they already know too much, then I'm going to need a little more time getting ready."

Daniel kissed me. "Take as much time as you need," he said. "I'll get the driver to go extra fast if we need."

I laughed and shook my head. "All right, getting ready," I said, slipping out of bed.

I picked up my black dress where it had been discarded on the floor. I dragged it on over my head, smoothing the material down with my fingers. There were a couple of wrinkles from where it had been unceremoniously discarded, but I didn't think anyone would notice. More obnoxious was my hair. I dragged a comb through it for the second time that night and then carefully pinned it up.

"You look beautiful," Daniel said from behind me. He stepped closer, picking up my waiting necklace from the bedside table, and then put it on me, his fingers brushing lightly along my skin. "Absolutely beautiful."

I smiled at him in our reflection in the mirror. "Thank you," I told him. "You look nice as well."

Of course, we didn't really need to dress up to go over to Matt and Leanne's place. I knew that before the night was through, we would probably both end up on the living room floor, crawling around and playing with Zach and Layla. And I didn't look nearly as nice as I had that Friday evening when Daniel and I had gone on that great date, when I'd worn the sexy red dress that Leanne had helped me pick out.

But I liked the way that Daniel looked at me when I dressed like this. Of course, I could always see the tenderness in his gaze. And when we were having sex, I could see the raw desire reflected in his gaze as well. But this—this was something different. When he wanted me but knew that he couldn't have me, at least not yet, not until the end of the night? Daniel's gaze turned positively hungry.

"Anyway, I'm excited to tell Leanne all about our trip," I told Daniel as we headed down to the car.

"I'm just excited to be on our trip already," Daniel joked. "A little alone time with you, no other responsibilities on my plate for the time being. Just giving you pleasure."

I groaned. "Don't make me think about that right now," I begged him. "I don't even think I could cum anymore right now, but the last thing I need is to spend the whole dinner thinking about the ways that you plan to pleasure me."

Daniel laughed, slinging an arm around my shoulders and holding me close. "All right, deal," he told me.

When we got to Matt and Leanne's house, I headed for the kitchen to see if Leanne needed any help with anything. "Would you mind setting the table for me?" she asked over her shoulder.

"No problem," I said, smiling at her. Layla wandered into the kitchen to help me, and I couldn't stop thinking about how much this was just like how I had been as a kid, helping out my mom with setting the table.

Would I have that one day as well? A daughter of my own to help me set the table?

I could hear Daniel and Zach in the other room, peals of laughter coming from both of them as they played whatever it was that they were playing at the moment.

Would I have that one day as well? A son of my own that Daniel would play with, to keep him from getting underfoot in the kitchen while I worked to put the finishing touches on dinner?

When I looked up, Leanne was smiling knowingly at me. I remembered our conversation from earlier in the week, about how I needed to talk to Daniel about the important things at some point. Children was definitely something for us to talk about. There were other things, too, of course, but that was a big one. Fortunately, I was pretty sure we were on the same page about it.

Maybe this trip would give us the opportunity to talk about all of it. Not that I wanted to possibly spoil the trip with difficult conversations about our future, but we'd see if things would come up naturally, maybe.

"I haven't talked to him yet," I told Leanne, and she laughed.

"All right," she said easily. "But I can tell exactly what you're thinking."

"What, Mom?" Layla interrupted suddenly, looking back and forth between me and her mother. She was definitely getting to that age where it was more difficult to talk around her. Things didn't go over her head quite as easily. Gosh, was she really already six? Where had the time gone? "What is Auntie Abby thinking?"

I put a hand on Layla's head. "I'm just thinking about how great you are at setting the table," I said. "That's all."

Layla puffed up with pride, and Leanne smiled over at me.

If you had asked me, back before I met Daniel, I would have told you that I didn't want kids. It wasn't that I had never considered having kids before, because I definitely had. And it wasn't that I didn't like children.

No, it was that I had never met a man before who I could treat like an equal. I had never met a man who would be my partner, someone to help me with raising the kids. And I couldn't imagine raising kids on my own. I knew plenty of women did it every single day, but with my career hopes, it just had seemed out of the question.

Now, though, things were different. In such a short time, Daniel had upended my worldview. Made me realize that maybe I could find that man who was the perfect match for me. The man who would be there by my side forever if I would let him. The man who would be worth any drama or heartache or anything else.

There was no one else I would rather spend the rest of my life with.

I thought back to the rest of the conversation I had had with Leanne. About how I was afraid to even think about the future, afraid to think of what I wanted in my life. That was all because of Daniel, because everything that I wanted came back to him eventually.

But suddenly, I realized I wasn't as afraid of it all as I had been before. Maybe it had something to do with this trip that Daniel was planning for us. Or maybe it just had something to do with how much time Daniel and I had been spending together lately. We had been practically inseparable ever since we had made up after our fight. Not codependent or anything, never that. We both had our lives. I had gone out to see Leanne for drinks on Tuesday, and we had gone out with Austin on Thursday night for drinks and a few rounds of darts.

Things had been great between us, though, and I could only see them getting better in the future. A future that maybe I was ready to start planning now.

I smiled to myself as the boys came into the kitchen.

"What are you thinking about?" Daniel asked in an undertone as he sat down beside me.

I grinned over at him. "Just about how lucky I am to have all of this," I said, squeezing his thigh meaningfully so he would know that I wasn't just talking about Matt and Leanne and their family. No, he was part of all this, and I was lucky to have him as well. Especially in light of everything that had happened between the two of us.

Daniel smiled back at me, leaning in to quickly brush his lips against mine, as the kids both chorused noisy *ewws*. He laughed as he pulled away. "Sorry," he said, looking entirely unrepentant. I couldn't help but giggle as Leanne rolled her eyes fondly at us.

Chapter 25

Daniel

I WAS STILL SURPRISED by how much at home I felt around Matt and Leanne and their family. Especially since I had never really had much of a family life of my own, and since I had been living on my own since Austin moved out, I just felt like it shouldn't be this easy to slip into this new role. But they all made it easy for me.

I felt at home here, in a way that still shocked me. But then again, I supposed it was no surprise, really, with the way that Abby could somehow, with just her presence, make my own house feel so much more like a home.

That wasn't the only thing I liked about Abby, of course, but that was definitely part of it. The fact that we already felt like family, the fact that she and her family had so easily opened up to me and let me become a part of their lives. I felt whole in a way I had never felt before. Like nothing was missing from my life, like I wasn't yearning for some other deeper purpose or something else in my life.

"Leanne, wonderful dinner as always," I said when I was a few bites into my food.

Leanne laughed. "You don't have to say that every time you're here," she said to me. "This is just pasta. A pretty simple pasta, at that."

"Still," I said, shrugging at her. I glanced over at Abby, grinning sheepishly. "As Abby can tell you, I don't do a lot of cooking for myself. Breakfasts a lot of days, but by the time I get home from work, I just don't have the will or the energy to get too fancy with dinner. A good, warm, home-cooked meal is still special for me."

"You two should come over more for family dinners," Leanne said, laughing. "And Abby, I think that's a request from your man for you to do a little more cooking at home."

Abby laughed, but I shook my head. "That wouldn't be fair," I said. "Abby stays at the office as long as I do every day. I keep trying to shoo her out early, but she won't go."

Leanne grinned at Abby, who shrugged. "I'm not going to let him be the last person in the office," she said. "Especially not every day."

"Sounds like you're both too competitive for your own good," Matt joked. "There's this thing called relaxation, you know."

Abby smiled broadly. "We'll be getting plenty of that soon enough," she assured her brother. She looked excitedly back and forth between the two of them. "Daniel's decided to push back our meetings for a little while so that he and I can go traveling. We're leaving on the twenty-first for Bangkok!"

"That's amazing!" Leanne said in surprise. "The twenty-first, though? Of this month? That's so soon! Why didn't you tell me sooner than that? We'll have to have a going away party and everything. How long are you going to be gone for?"

Abby laughed at all the questions. "We just planned it," she said. "It's kind of a spontaneous trip," she added.

"I'll say," Leanne said. "I mean, I knew that you always wanted to go traveling, but I didn't realize you were able to take the time off from work right now. Especially not both of you."

"We'll probably have to do a little bit of work while we're on the road," I explained. "Erin, my assistant, is going to be looking after things around the office, keeping us informed of the most important bits, the stuff that Abby and I can't delegate. We might even do a few remote video conference calls and that sort of thing while we're over there."

Initially when I had talked to Erin about leaving for this trip, I had tried to arrange things so that we wouldn't need to do any of the work while we were on the road. But modern technology being what it was these days, I was quickly starting to realize that there was no reason why the business had to stagnate while we traveled around the globe. And if we were able to strike some sort of balance between our travel and the business side of things, then it could only prolong our trip.

Besides, I kind of liked the idea of Abby and I curled up in our bungalow in Thailand, working away at our computers, before we tumbled back in bed together, unable to deny the chemistry between us any longer.

"We don't know how long we'll be gone for either," Abby added, looking almost nervous. She glanced toward the kids and then back to her brother and Leanne. I knew she wouldn't want to be gone for too long. She wouldn't want to miss anything in their lives. But at the same time, I wanted to show her everything I could during our trip. Maybe a few scheduled breaks, come back home for a bit and get some real work done in the office. We could always leave again.

I filed that idea away to think about later.

"For now, we're just trying to plan as little as possible," I told them.

Matt looked wary. "You do at least have someplace to stay when you arrive in Thailand, don't you?" he asked, bringing home to me the fact that Abby was his *little* sister. I no longer worried that Matt wouldn't accept me as a suitable match for his sister. We were beyond that point. But he would always be protective of her. He would always do his best to look out for her. And he wasn't quite to the point, yet, of realizing that I would sooner cut off one of my limbs than let anything happen to Abby.

Abby was laughing, though. "Yeah, we have a place to stay," she said. "We've actually only have one night in Bangkok, and then we're headed down south to the islands. We're staying at this amazing resort there, bungalows out over the water, a really special place. It's going to be five whole days of luxury and massages."

"You're making me jealous," Leanne said, laughing.

"You're making *me* jealous," Matt echoed, "and I can't even remember the last time I had a massage!"

"But then after that, we don't know where we're going. And we also don't know how long the trip will end up being," Abby continued. She smiled over at me. "We're just going with how we feel. I'd really like to get to Australia at some point, but we'll see."

Leanne sighed wistfully. "That sounds amazing," she said. "Even if you do have to work along the way."

"Right?" Abby said. "Like, I don't even care if I have to bring my laptop with me; I'm going to Thailand." She turned to her niece and nephew, smiling at them. "That's in Asia," she explained to them. "And guess what? When we're done with the beaches in the south, we'll probably head north and get to feed elephants and give them baths and everything."

"And ride them?" Layla asked, her eyes shining.

"Probably not ride one," Abby said, shaking her head, "but we will be close enough to pet them. How cool is that?"

"Can I come with you?" Zach asked. "I can fit in your suitcase."

Abby laughed. "I don't think it would be a very comfortable flight like that," she said. "And it's a long flight, too. Like, hours and hours and hours. Longer than when you guys flew to California."

Zach wrinkled his nose. "Yuck," he said.

"Yuck," Layla agreed, but I could tell she was still thinking about elephants. I made a mental note to try to find her a souvenir from Thailand with elephants on it.

"Well, it definitely sounds like quite the trip," Matt said, smiling at the two of us. "Try and let me know where you're staying if you can. I know that you're probably sharing all that information with the office anyway, but I would just hate it if something were to happen to you and we didn't know it."

"Of course," Abby said, nodding emphatically.

"I've already given your contact information to Erin as well," I promised him. "So if anything comes up, she'll be able to get in touch."

"And I'll give you Erin's number, too," Abby added. "So if you need to get in touch with us, you can do it that way."

"Perfect," Matt said, nodding approvingly.

Leanne sighed. "I wish we could do a trip like that," she said. "But it's so hard with the kids in school for most of the year. And when they're not in school, that's always peak travel times, either summer or the holidays, which makes it hard to book anything."

I grinned at her. "Maybe next time I'll take you all on vacation," I said, only half-joking. We probably wouldn't go anywhere as exotic as Thailand with the kids, and of course we would want to plan everything in advance. But I could see it already. Maybe a trip to Disney, or a big camping trip. The kind of trip I had always wanted to take as a kid but never got to. My own family hadn't been anything like this.

Matt shook his head. "You don't have to—" he started to say.

"I know," I interrupted. "And I'm not making any promises." I glanced over at Abby, seeing the way she was smiling at me. I squeezed her knee lightly. "But I think it would be a lot of fun. So we should think about this in the future."

"But for now, one trip at a time," Abby said, saving me from the hole I was surely digging for myself.

"One trip at a time," Leanne echoed, but I could see the happiness in her eyes.

"You know, I regret ever telling you not to date this guy," Matt joked. Everyone laughed. His face turned serious. "The biggest benefit I see is the light in my sister's eyes. She practically glows with happiness and that's something worth celebrating." He cleared his throat. "And may your relationship last forever so we can all reap the benefits." More laughter erupted around the table.

I smiled around at them, listening to Leanne and Abby chat about all the things we should make sure to do while we were in Thailand.

Whatever we ended up doing on the trip, I realized, I was the happiest I had ever been. Blood relations or not, these people sitting around the table here were my family, and I loved each and every one of them. I never wanted to imagine a life without them.

Chapter 26

Abby

I COULDN'T BELIEVE how soon it was before Daniel's and my trip. In terms of the trip itself, things were going swimmingly. It helped that we didn't want to plan too much of it in advance. I had done a little bit of research to see what other things I might want to do in Thailand, but we weren't worrying about booking transportation or accommodations just yet.

I wasn't even too worried about packing. I had read that it would be cheap and easy to buy clothing once we arrived there, and anyway, the clothing I could find there would probably be more suitable to the hot and humid climate than anything I could bring with me. I was looking forward to doing a little shopping, too. Maybe I could find something pretty to bring back for Leanne.

But the tricky part was getting the office ready for Daniel's and my departure. Daniel hadn't made up huge mounds of printouts and notes for Erin like he had for me. First of all, she wouldn't be stepping into the role of interim CEO. But second of all, Erin informed me that the only reason she had agreed to take on more of a role at the office at all was because Daniel had promised he wouldn't leave her all those notes to go through.

Smart girl, I thought. But then again, she also knew more about the company than I did, since she had been there for longer and had worked closely with Daniel for all of her time there with McGregor Enterprises.

Of course, I was definitely starting to catch up to her. Daniel had ramped up his CEO training plans, which surprised me to be honest. I figured that since we were going to be taking time away from the office, we would quit the training now and pick up with it when we got back. After all, it wasn't like Daniel and I didn't have plenty of other things to get in order before we left.

But the way he had sped up the learning process made me wonder. Just what kind of business relationship did he see for us when we returned from this trip? Would I still be welcome back to work for his company? Or was he hoping that this time away would strengthen our relationship and weaken our work ties? Did he want me to go to work for a different company when I returned?

I knew this was all stuff I needed to talk to Daniel about. It wasn't healthy to keep these concerns to myself. But I just couldn't seem to find a good time to talk to him about any of it. When we were at the office, there were dozens of last-minute meetings and things to attend to. And when we were at home, we were either discussing the trip or else thinking about anything and everything except for work.

I didn't want to ruin things. I didn't want to jeopardize our trip. Not that I really believed I would. But still, I was afraid to ask too many questions. I was afraid to make it seem like I didn't trust him to make the right decisions for the good of the company as well as our relationship.

"What are you looking so pensive about?" Daniel asked from behind me.

I startled, jumping about a foot into the air. Then, I turned sheepishly toward him. "I'm just waiting for the coffee to be done," I said, gesturing to the pot in front of me.

Daniel frowned. "Sure," he said. "But I can tell you're thinking pretty hard as well. Are you nervous about our trip?"

"Something like that," I admitted. I shrugged. "We just have so much to get done before then." It was sort of a lie, or at least a shading of the truth, but I didn't know how to tell him what I was really worried about. If he didn't want me to come back to work for him once our trip was over, I would just have to wait and deal with it then. No sense panicking before I even knew what might happen.

After all, hadn't I learned that lesson when we had fought post-trial? I had come up with so many horrible ideas of what Daniel might think of me, I had been so sure that he would fire me and that he would never want anything to do with me again. But none of those things had come to pass.

"Don't worry about it," Daniel said, grinning at me. "I appreciate all the help you've been giving me in getting all the last-minute things done, but at the end of the day, I don't want you to be worried about it."

"It is your company," I joked weakly. "I guess I should leave the worrying to the boss."

Daniel frowned thoughtfully at that. "Can you come back to my office with me?" he asked, pouring us each a mug of coffee once the pot finally finished brewing.

"Sure thing," I said, wondering what else he was going to add to my plate that day. I knew that I shouldn't have been loitering around the break room like that, but I just had to step away from it all for a moment.

I followed him back to his office, though, knowing that whatever he was delegating to me, he must have a dozen other more challenging things on his plate for the day. He didn't delegate lightly; I knew that about him.

I was surprised when he closed and locked the door behind us. I raised an eyebrow at him. "I thought we didn't do that kind of stuff around the office," I reminded him, even though just the suggestion of a heavy make-out session, and maybe more, made me want to throw the rule book out the window just then. We'd both been so exhausted in the evenings that week that we had pretty much just been collapsing into bed with each other. My body ached to feel him inside of me again.

But Daniel shook his head. "I just want to make sure we're not disturbed," he said. "I have something serious I want to discuss with you."

I felt my blood run cold. Had I done something wrong? Was he calling off this whole trip before we had even gone anywhere?

Daniel was grinning at me, though. "Relax," he said. "It's not a bad thing. In fact, it could be a very good thing for both of us. Why don't you sit down?"

I slowly walked over to the chair at the far side of his desk. "What's going on?" I asked him.

"It's about the business," Daniel said. "I brought you into this company as my advisor, in part because that was the role that Gerrard had always filled, and the one that I thought I was trying to find a replacement for. But I'm beginning to realize that that position title doesn't do justice to the work you've been putting into the job in your time here."

"Okay," I said slowly, my mind trying furiously to process that. It must just be some sort of HR thing. Restructuring of the company or something. A different title for me, no longer Daniel's advisor, but still with all the same responsibilities as before. I wondered why he looked so serious about that, though. And why he felt the need to tell me it himself, rather than letting HR handle it.

But Daniel's next words shocked me. "I was wondering, actually, if you'd like to be my partner within the company. Rather than my advisor, you'd be a co-CEO, and as the company grows, you'll have the ability to take on whatever projects you'd like."

I gaped at him, unable to find the words. Co-CEO? Had he really said that? I was tempted to remind him of the mistake I had made when I was filling in for him before. But I knew I needed to let that go. The situation with Duncan had been resolved by me firing him as our client. He had never even gone to the news with anything he had heard, or if he had, no one had been able to use any of it. The story had totally fizzled out. No harm, no foul.

Besides, Daniel had been training me to be a CEO for real, ever since the Duncan debacle. I knew so much more about McGregor Enterprises already, and I would only learn more the longer I spent at the company and the more I got my hands dirty with different CEO projects.

I remembered what Daniel had said last time, about how he wouldn't have asked me to stand in for him if he didn't trust my ability to do the job. I had to assume that it was the same now. He believed that I could do the job. And not only that, but he was willing to work alongside me. Give me partnership in his company.

I found myself nodding before I was even aware of my answer. But still, I couldn't help asking, "Are you sure, though?"

Daniel nodded at me. "I want to do this together," he said. "I want to share our legacy."

It was those simple words—our legacy—that really did it for me. I was still stunned, but I could feel a quick rush of elation flash through me as well. I practically jumped over his desk to throw my arms around him. We kissed messily, both overcome by our emotions.

"I take it that's a yes?" Daniel asked amusedly as I finally released him.

I realized only then that I still had yet to say a word to him. "Yes," I said breathlessly, bobbing my head. "Yes. One hundred times over, yes."

Daniel laughed, pulling me into another kiss. "Good," he said fiercely as I pulled away. "Because I know how much it means to you to become a CEO, and there's no way in hell I'm letting you go to work for another company. You're mine, Abby James."

I shivered at the possessive tone to his voice. But I didn't mind the idea of belonging to him, or of becoming a co-CEO of his company. In fact, it sounded pretty much perfect. "And here I was, worried that the reason that you were working so hard to train me up was that when we came back from this trip, you were going to recommend that I go to work somewhere else," I joked.

Daniel's arms tightened around me, pulling me down into his lap. "Absolutely not," he said, shaking his head. "I just wanted to make sure that you were all ready to take over the role I envisioned for you. And that you weren't going to have to be stressed while we're in Thailand. I wanted you to have all the on the job training that you needed before we leave home."

"Thanks again for trusting me. And for giving me this chance," I said quietly. "You don't know how grateful I am."

"I think I have an idea," Daniel said, grinning up at me. "But if you really want to show me how grateful you are, then by all means." His face reddened as if he'd just realized he'd said the words out loud. He cleared his throat. "I was just kidding. That just came out really scumbag sounding. I totally didn't mean it like that—"

"You don't have to apologize," I teased. "Now it sounds like your begging."

"I'm not..." His voice trailed off, as if he wasn't sure himself.

I glanced toward the door, but knew it was locked. This was usually so off-limits for us. And there was a reason for that. But then again, everyone in the office knew we were dating already. Nor would it be unusual for me and Daniel to be there in his office together, behind closed doors. We worked together. They would all just assume that we were discussing an upcoming business strategy or a deal or something. Or that we were maybe on a conference call together.

We could do this, if we wanted to. And right then, I realized that I really, really wanted to.

I slid off Daniel's lap, kneeling gracefully between his legs, running my hands up his thick, muscular thighs and reaching for his belt. I licked my lips, watching as Daniel's eyes darkened, his cock twitching in his pants. But before I could push his pants and boxers out of the way, long before I could get my mouth on him, there was a knock at the door.

I groaned silently, putting my head down against Daniel's leg. What a time to be interrupted. It was like the universe wanted to keep us on edge. To force us to stick to the rules that we had set out what felt like so long ago now. But I knew we had no choice but to answer it.

I sighed and pushed myself to my feet. "Tonight," I promised Daniel in a low voice. "When we're home alone. I promise I'll show you just how grateful I am." My voice was already husky and raw with desire, as though I'd already had his length in my mouth for hours on end.

Daniel grimaced but nodded at me, redoing his belt buckle. He cleared his throat awkwardly. "Would you answer that? I'm a little..." He trailed off, gesturing toward the obvious tent in the front of his slacks.

I smirked at him and headed for the door. When I opened it, Erin was standing there, and I could tell from the sly grin on her face that she had some idea of exactly what she had interrupted. She wasn't just here to keep us from doing lewd things in the office, though. She had a stack of documents in one hand.

"These are for you, Daniel," she said as I stepped back to let her into the office. "It's the notes on our latest business undertakings, just like you asked for. Progress for each of the projects, earnings projections, all that sort of thing."

Daniel nodded and then tipped his head toward me. "Why don't you give those to my partner, the new co-CEO of McGregor Enterprises," he said smoothly. "She'll make sure it's all spick and span."

The grin on Erin's face widened as she turned toward me. "Co-CEO, huh?" she asked. "Congratulations! I guess those are the perks of sleeping with the boss?"

I blushed horribly, even though I knew she meant it as a joke. I knew that was exactly the line that the media was going to take when they found out about my promotion. That the only reason I had risen in the company was because Daniel and I were dating. Well, I'd just have to show all of them. I was here because of my hard work, dedication, and intelligence.

Sleeping with Daniel was just an added bonus.

Still, the smile on Erin's face and the quick hug that she gave me soothed my indignation at those words. "You deserve it for putting up with him," she teased.

Daniel raised his eyebrow at Erin, but he didn't seem offended either. In fact, it was the most relaxed I had seen him around his employees since I had first started working there. Maybe people really could change over time.

"Careful, Erin," he said mock warningly. "Even when we go off to Thailand, remember that I'm still your boss."

Erin gave him an ironic bow and backed toward the door. "So true, boss," she said, smirk still firmly in place. She winked at me. "Abby, let me know if you have any questions as you're going over all of that."

"Will do," I said, grinning at her.

She shut the door on the way out. For a moment, I was tempted to go lock it again, return to my spot on the floor between Daniel's legs. But then I looked down at the papers in my hand and remembered all the other work I wanted to get done that day. I sighed. "Tonight," I promised Daniel again.

He laughed easily. "Tonight," he agreed, nodding at me. "And same thing that Erin said, let me know if you need any help with anything. I don't want you feeling overwhelmed. You've been doing such a great job lately, and I want to keep that going if we can."

"Thanks," I said gratefully. "I'll see you in a little while for that meeting with the shareholders."

"By the way," Daniel said as I started to leave the room.

"Yeah?" I asked over my shoulder.

"You're going to need an office if you're co-CEO," Daniel continued. "But unfortunately, this building is rather limited on office space.

So I was thinking that we might need to move buildings, although that seems like a lot of work, or else...you might just have to share this office with me. What do you think? We could get one of those his-and-hers desks, me on one side and you on the other."

My grin felt wide enough to split my face in two. "That sounds perfect," I told him. "And there'll be plenty of time for you to hire someone to set that up while we're on our trip!"

The idea of being co-CEO was still intimidating, no matter how much I had learned from Daniel since I had come to work for McGregor Enterprises. But it definitely helped to know that he would be there by my side, every step of the way.

Chapter 27

Daniel

I STRETCHED HUGELY as I lay on top of the bed in our luxurious hotel room. Thailand was definitely agreeing with me, I decided. I couldn't remember the last time I had felt this relaxed. I rolled my head to the side so I could look toward the broad terrace. The curtains were blowing in with the breeze, and I could just see Abby's silhouette as she leaned against the railing, looking down at the jungle far below.

I knew Abby had been partial to the pretty bungalow we had stayed on for our first nights down in the islands, but personally, I was happy to come here and have such privacy. We were the only people on this level of the lodge, and no one would be able to see out onto our terrace or its plunge pool. There was a certain level of exaggerated comfort to this place that had been missing from our previous accommodations. I loved it.

I headed out onto the terrace. The water in the plunge pool was perfectly still, and the afternoon air was hot and humid. Abby didn't move as I walked out to her, leaning against her, putting one hand on either side of hers where they rested against the railing. I slowly lowered my mouth, kissing her shoulders and her neck.

She was dressed in only a flimsy cover-up, with no swimsuit underneath. After all, it wasn't like anyone could see us except for the birds in the sky. I myself wasn't wearing anything after the nap I'd had, passed out on the bed. It had been a long and slow trip to get here, to the far north of Thailand and this quiet, peaceful retreat.

This privacy—it was another thing I had been missing with our bungalow. Sure, we'd had our bungalow all to ourselves, but there hadn't really been anywhere else that we could retreat to privately at that resort. Here, we had much more space to just enjoy one another.

And right now, my prick was already stiff with how badly I wanted to enjoy Abby's body. I rocked against her, my length sliding down the cleft of her ass as she pushed back against me. She turned in my arms, leaning her mouth up so that she could kiss me. Her fingers trailed down my naked body. She cupped my erection in her hand, squeezing lightly, making me groan. I thrust into the circle of her fist, using her for release.

She dropped down to her knees gracefully, bringing my tip to her lips. She flicked her tongue out, licking at the bead of precum dotting my slit. Then, she wrapped her lips around my head, bobbing up and down in practiced movements, her other hand coming up to play with my balls all the while.

I groaned, leaning back against the railing, my head falling back. One of my hands came up to caress Abby's soft hair, tangling in the errant strands that had escape from her long blonde braid. I didn't know if I had been dreaming about her during my nap or if it was just that talented mouth of hers, but I was quickly close to the edge. I wanted this to last a little while longer, though.

I pressed against her shoulder to get her to stop. She pulled off with a *pop*, smirking up at me as I sank down to join her on the cool tiles of the terrace. I lay back on the rug that was spread there, and she climbed on top of me, wasting no time before lowering herself down onto my needy member. I caught her hips, guiding them with my hands. Not that she needed any guidance. She sank down onto me again and again, shifting slightly to change the angle each time.

Suddenly, she gasped, her fingers finding mine at her hips, scrabbling for a grip. "Right there, right there," she whimpered, her movements becoming frenzied as she chased her orgasm. The more I watched her fall apart above me, the more difficult it was to keep from tumbling over that edge myself. She was shaking with desire, her body slick with sweat as my fingers trailed along her sides and cupped her breasts and then her ass.

She slumped forward, pushing her hair impatiently back so that she could look down at me with those bewitching eyes of hers. She slammed down on my length again and again, and I could tell that we were both so close.

I kissed the inside of her wrist, where she had her hands planted on either side of my head. She whimpered as I raked my teeth lightly over her pulse point. I could see the goose bumps there in her sensitive skin. She collapsed over me, and I wrapped my arms around her, holding her close, thrusting up into her when it became clear that she was too overcome to continue her own movements.

We came together, bodies slick with heat, pleasure bursting through our veins. It felt like we were suspended there forever, just the two of us in this jungle in Thailand, the birds flying overhead. My body spent itself over and over, wave after wave of my seed spurting into her, as her walls milked me for all I was worth.

I could barely remember who I was, just lost there in the sensation of utter bliss, sure that that only thing that mattered in this world right now was this beautiful woman in my arms.

Slowly, I came back into myself, separating from her, letting her pull off of me and lay down at my side. "I love you," Abby murmured after a long moment, as her fingers trailed aimless patterns on my chest. I could sense, however, that there was a "but" there. Sure enough: "But these tiles are really uncomfortable. Can we move in to the bed or something?"

I rolled swiftly to my feet and then bent down and scooped her up into my arms as she shrieked with laughter. "You always do that," she giggled as I deposited her on the bed and crawled after her.

I shrugged unrepentantly and pulled her back into my arms. "That better?" I asked her.

"Mmm," Abby hummed, nuzzling my shoulder.

"For the record, I love you, too," I told her, and she giggled again. I put a finger beneath her chin, tilting her face up so she was looking at me. "In fact," I said seriously, "I love you so much that I'd like you to move in with me when we get back to Chicago. If you're okay with that."

Abby snorted, a huge grin on her face. "I've been waiting for you to ask that for ages," she said, and I had to laugh.

"Oh yeah?" I said. "Well, I have another question for you." I rolled away from her and grabbed my discarded trousers, pulling the small, black velvet box out of the pocket. I turned back toward the bed, where Abby was sitting up now, looking curious.

Slowly, I dropped down on one knee. "Abby James, will you marry me?" I asked. "I can't imagine my life without you, either at home or around the office. And I know that I've already secured the future of your working alongside me, at least for a little while until your contract is up, but I don't want to be without you for a single day outside of work either."

Abby's eyes lit up, and she nodded, putting a hand over her mouth. I could see tears in her eyes. Happy tears, I supposed. "Oh Daniel, yes," she said, the tears overflowing into two crystalline streams that flowed down her cheeks.

I took her trembling hand, sliding the beautiful antique ring onto her third finger. "It was my mother's once," I told Abby. "I never got the chance to know her well, but I think she would have approved of you."

Abby's smile was dazzling as I reached up to brush away the tear tracks. She leaned down and kissed me deeply, passion spilling over from her lips to mine and vice versa.

"I do," she said quietly as we broke apart.

I laughed and gave her shoulder a small shove. "I don't think we're quite to that point in our story just yet," I told her. "But we'll set the date soon, I promise."

Abby giggled for a long moment, reaching for my hands and pulling me up onto the bed. "All right, smart-ass," she said.

"And I guess we'd better start scouting for wedding locations as well," I said. "I think we'll have to be married here in Thailand now, in light of this history. So find somewhere that you really want Matt and Leanne and the kids to see."

Abby grinned and leaned in for another kiss that quickly turned into something more. "Mrs. Abby McGregor," she said quietly afterward, just as she was drifting off to sleep. I kissed her forehead and tried to memorize that smile on her face and the feeling of her body against mine. This was something I never could have imagined I would get in life, more perfect that I could ever have hoped for.

THE END

Counting the Billions Series

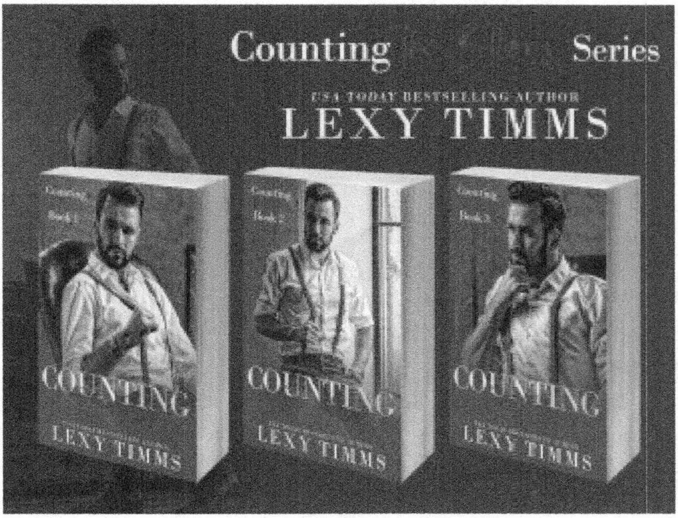

Book 1 – Counting the Days
Book 2 – Counting on You
Book 3 – Counting the Kisses

Find Lexy Timms:

LEXY TIMMS NEWSLETTER:

http://eepurl.com/9i0vD

Lexy Timms Facebook Page:

https://www.facebook.com/SavingForever

Lexy Timms Website:

http://www.lexytimms.com

BOSS
BOSS
BOSS
Lexy
Timms
Managing
BOSSES
Lexy
Timms
FREE
for a
Limited
Time

Want

FREE READS?

Sign up for Lexy Timms' newsletter
And she'll send you updates on new releases,
ARC copies of books and a whole lotta fun!

Sign up for news and updates!
http://eepurl.com/9i0vD

More by Lexy Timms:

FROM BEST SELLING AUTHOR, Lexy Timms, comes a billionaire romance that'll make you swoon and fall in love all over again.

Jamie Connors has given up on men. Despite being smart, pretty, and just slightly overweight, she's a magnet for the kind of guys that don't stay around.

Her sister's wedding is at the foreground of the family's attention. Jamie would be fine with it if her sister wasn't pressuring her to lose weight so she'll fit in the maid of honor dress, her mother would get off her case and her ex-boyfriend wasn't about to become her brother-in-law.

Determined to step out on her own, she accepts a PA position from billionaire Alex Reid. The job includes an apartment on his property and gets her out of living in her parents' basement.

Jamie must balance her life and somehow figure out how to manage her billionaire boss, without falling in love with him.

** The Boss is book 1 in the Managing the Bosses series. All your questions won't be answered in the first book. It may end on a cliff hanger.

For mature audiences only. There are adult situations, but this is a love story, NOT erotica.

FRAGILE TOUCH

"HIS BODY IS PERFECT. He's got this face that isn't just heart-melting but actually kind of exotic..."

Lillian Warren's life is just how she's designed it. She has a high-paying job working with celebrities and the elite, teaching them how to better organize their lives. She's on her own, the days quiet, but she likes it that way. Especially since she's still figuring out how to live with her recent diagnosis of Crohn's disease. Her cats keep her company, and she's not the least bit lonely.

Fun-loving personal trainer, Cayden, thinks his neighbor is a killjoy. He's only seen her a few times, and the woman looks like she needs a drink or three. He knows how to party and decides to invite her to over—if he can find her. What better way to impress her than take care of her overgrown yard? She proceeds to thank him by throwing up in his painstakingly-trimmed-to-perfection bushes.

Something about the fragile, mysterious woman captivates him.

Something about this rough-on-the-outside bear of a man attracts Lily, despite her heart warning her to tread carefully.

Faking It Description:

HE GROANED. THIS WAS torture. Being trapped in a room with a beautiful woman was just about every man's fantasy, but he had to remember that this was just pretend.

Allyson Smith has crushed on her boss for years, but never dared to make a move. When she finds herself without a date to her brother's upcoming wedding, Allyson tells her family one innocent white lie: that she's been dating her boss. Unfortunately, her boss discovers her lie, and insists on posing as her boyfriend to escort her to the wedding.

Playboy billionaire Dane Prescott always has a new heiress on his arm, but he can't get his assistant Allyson out of his head. He's fought his attraction to her, until he gets caught up in her scheme of a fake relationship.

One passionate weekend with the boss has Allyson Smith questioning everything she believes in. Falling for a wealthy playboy like Dane is against the rules, but if she's just faking it what's the harm?

Capturing Her Beauty

KAYLA REID HAS ALWAYS been into fashion and everything to do with it. Growing up wasn't easy for her. A bigger girl trying to squeeze into the fashion world is like trying to suck an entire gelatin mold through a straw; possible, but difficult.

She found herself an open door as a designer and jumped right in. Her designs always made the models smile. The colors, the fabrics, the styles. Never once did she dream of being on the other side of the lens. She got to watch her clothing strut around on others and that was good enough.

But who says you can't have a little fun when you're off the clock?

Sometimes trying on the latest fashions is just as good as making them. Kayla's hours in front of the mirror were a guilty pleasure.

A chance meeting with one of the company photographers may turn into more than just an impromptu photo shoot.

Hot n' Handsome, Rich & Single... how far are you willing to go?
MEET ALEX REID, CEO of Reid Enterprise. Billionaire extraordinaire, chiseled to perfection, panty-melter and currently single.

Learn about Alex Reid before he began Managing the Bosses. Alex Reid sits down for an interview with R&S.

His life style is like his handsome looks: hard, fast, breath-taking and out to play ball. He's risky, charming and determined.

How close to the edge is Alex willing to go? Will he stop at nothing to get what he wants?

Alex Reid is book 1 in the R&S Rich and Single Series. Fall in love with these hot and steamy men; all single, successful, and searching for love.

Book One is FREE!

SOMETIMES THE HEART needs a different kind of saving... find out if Charity Thompson will find a way of saving forever in this hospital setting Best-Selling Romance by Lexy Timms

Charity Thompson wants to save the world, one hospital at a time. Instead of finishing med school to become a doctor, she chooses a different path and raises money for hospitals – new wings, equipment, whatever they need. Except there is one hospital she would be happy to never set foot in again—her father's. So of course, he hires her to create a gala for his sixty-fifth birthday. Charity can't say no. Now she is working in the one place she doesn't want to be. Except she's attracted to Dr. Elijah Bennet, the handsome playboy chief.

Will she ever prove to her father that's she's more than a med school dropout? Or will her attraction to Elijah keep her from repairing the one thing she desperately wants to fix?

HEART OF THE BATTLE Series

In a world plagued with darkness, she would be his salvation.

No one gave Erik a choice as to whether he would fight or not. Duty to the crown belonged to him, his father's legacy remaining beyond the grave.

Taken by the beauty of the countryside surrounding her, Linzi would do anything to protect her father's land. Britain is under attack and Scotland is next. At a time she should be focused on suitors, the men of her country have gone to war and she's left to stand alone.

Love will become available, but will passion at the touch of the enemy unravel her strong hold first?

THE RECRUITING TRIP

Aspiring college athlete Aileen Nessa is finding the recruiting process beyond daunting. Being ranked #10 in the world for the 100m hurdles at the age of eighteen is not a fluke, even though she believes that one race, where everything clicked magically together, might be. American universities don't seem to think so. Letters are pouring in from all over the country.

As she faces the challenge of differentiating between a college's genuine commitment to her or just empty promises from talent-seeking coaches, Aileen heads to the University of Gatica, a Division One school, on a recruiting trip. Her best friend dares her to go just to see the cute guys on the school's brochure.

The university's athletic program boasts one of the top hurdlers in the country. Tyler Jensen is the school's NCAA champion in the hurdles and Jim Thorpe recipient for top defensive back in football. His incredible blue-green eyes, confident smile and rock hard six pack abs mess with Aileen's concentration.

His offer to take her under his wing, should she choose to come to Gatica, is a temping proposition that has her wondering if she might be with an angel or making a deal with the devil himself.

THE ONE YOU CAN'T FORGET

Emily Rose Dougherty is a good Catholic girl from mythical Walkerville, CT. She had somehow managed to get herself into a heap trouble with the law, all because an ex-boyfriend has decided to make things difficult.

Luke "Spade" Wade owns a Motorcycle repair shop and is the Road Captain for Hades' Spawn MC. He's shocked when he reads in the paper that his old high school flame has been arrested. She's always been the one he couldn't forget.

Will destiny let them find each other again? Or what happened in the past, best left for the history books?

** *This is book 1 of the Hades' Spawn MC Series. All your questions may not be answered in the first book.*

FORTUNE RIDERS MC
BILLIONAIRE BIKER
LEXY TIMMS
Download For
FREE
Lexy
Timms

Fire HOUSE ROMANCE
CAUGHT in
FLAMES
BESTSELLING AUTHOR
LEXY TIMMS
LIMITED
TIME
Lexy
Timms
FREE
DOWNLOAD

ONE YOU CAN'T
Forget
LEXY TIMMS
Lexy
Timmins
Grab Your
FREE
Copy Today!

Lexy
Timms
THE BOSS
Lexy
Timms
Grab your
FREE
copy today!

FOREVER
FOREVER
FOREVER
BOOK 3
BOOK 2
BOOK 1
Lexy Timms
Saving
FOREVER
Lexy
Timms
Limited
Time for
99cents

Bestselling Author
LEXY TIMMS
BEATING THE Biker

LEXY TIMMS
MOMENT IN TIME: BOOK ONE
HIGHLANDERS
Bride

Don't miss out!

Visit the website below and you can sign up to receive emails whenever Lexy Timms publishes a new book. There's no charge and no obligation.

https://books2read.com/r/B-A-NNL-RKFW

BOOKS 2 READ

Connecting independent readers to independent writers.

Did you love *Counting the Kisses*? Then you should read *Kissed by Passion* by Lexy Timms!

"Love is blind, despite the world's attempt to give it eyes."

Phillip Greene is the shining resident at St. Joseph's Hospital. Lilly Carver is the personal assistant of her billionaire father at his finance firm.

Two different worlds, two different sets of rules.

But when their worlds collide, fires ignite. Forests are burned to the ground. And neither of their fathers approve of the union.

One reckless weekend threatens to tear them apart as their secretive affair surfaces. Can Phillip handle the paparazzi? Can they both convince their families how wrong they are to disapprove?

Or will the standards of their different worlds put out the fire sparking between them?

Love knows no color. No race. No limits.

Kissed by Billions Series
Book 1 – Kissed by Passion
Book 2 – Kissed by Desire
Book 3 – Kissed by Love
Read more at www.lexytimms.com.

Also by Lexy Timms

A Burning Love Series
Spark of Passion
Flame of Desire
Blaze of Ecstasy

A Chance at Forever Series
Forever Perfect
Forever Desired
Forever Together

BBW Romance Series
Capturing Her Beauty
Pursuing Her Dreams
Tracing Her Curves

Beating the Biker Series
Making Her His
Making the Break

Making of Them

Billionaire Banker Series

Banking on Him

Price of Passion

Investing in Love

Knowing Your Worth

Treasured Forever

Billionaire Holiday Romance Series

Driving Home for Christmas

The Valentine Getaway

Cruising Love

Billionaire in Disguise Series

Facade

Illusion

Charade

Billionaire Secrets Series

The Secret

Freedom

Courage

Trust

Impulse

Billionaire Secrets Box Set Books #1-3

Building Billions

Building Billions - Part 1

Building Billions - Part 2

Building Billions - Part 3

Conquering Warrior Series

Ruthless

Counting the Billions

Counting the Days

Counting On You

Counting the Kisses

Diamond in the Rough Anthology

Billionaire Rock

Billionaire Rock - part 2

Dominating PA Series

Her Personal Assistant - Part 1

Her Personal Assistant Box Set

Fake Billionaire Series

Faking It

Temporary CEO
Caught in the Act
Never Tell A Lie
Fake Christmas

Firehouse Romance Series
Caught in Flames
Burning With Desire
Craving the Heat
Firehouse Romance Complete Collection

For His Pleasure
Elizabeth
Georgia
Madison

Fortune Riders MC Series
Billionaire Biker
Billionaire Ransom
Billionaire Misery

Fragile Series
Fragile Touch
Fragile Kiss
Fragile Love

Hades' Spawn Motorcycle Club

One You Can't Forget

One That Got Away

One That Came Back

One You Never Leave

One Christmas Night

Hades' Spawn MC Complete Series

Hard Rocked Series

Rhyme

Harmony

Lyrics

Heart of Stone Series

The Protector

The Guardian

The Warrior

Heart of the Battle Series

Celtic Viking

Celtic Rune

Celtic Mann

Heart of the Battle Series Box Set

Heistdom Series

Master Thief

Goldmine

Diamond Heist

Smile For Me

Just About Series

About Love

About Truth

About Forever

Justice Series

Seeking Justice

Finding Justice

Chasing Justice

Pursuing Justice

Justice - Complete Series

Kissed by the Billionaire Series

Kissed by Passion

Love You Series

Love Life

Need Love

My Love

Managing the Billionaire

Never Enough

Managing the Bosses Series

The Boss

The Boss Too

Who's the Boss Now

Love the Boss

I Do the Boss

Wife to the Boss

Employed by the Boss

Brother to the Boss

Senior Advisor to the Boss

Forever the Boss

Christmas With the Boss

Billionaire in Control

Billionaire Makes Millions

Gift for the Boss - Novella 3.5

Managing the Bosses Box Set #1-3

Model Mayhem Series

Shameless

Modesty

Imperfection

Moment in Time

Highlander's Bride

Victorian Bride

Modern Day Bride

A Royal Bride

Forever the Bride

Outside the Octagon

Submit

Protecting Diana Series

Her Bodyguard

Her Defender

Her Champion

Her Protector

Her Forever

Protecting Layla Series

His Mission

His Objective

His Devotion

Racing Hearts Series

Rush

Pace
Fast

Reverse Harem Series
Primals
Archaic
Unitary

RIP Series
Track the Ripper
Hunt the Ripper
Pursue the Ripper

R&S Rich and Single Series
Alex Reid
Parker

Saving Forever
Saving Forever - Part 1
Saving Forever - Part 2
Saving Forever - Part 3
Saving Forever - Part 4
Saving Forever - Part 5
Saving Forever - Part 6
Saving Forever Part 7
Saving Forever - Part 8

Saving Forever Boxset Books #1-3

Shifting Desires Series

Jungle Heat

Jungle Fever

Jungle Blaze

Southern Romance Series

Little Love Affair

Siege of the Heart

Freedom Forever

Soldier's Fortune

Spelling Love Series

The Author

The Book Boyfriend

The Words of Love

Tattooist Series

Confession of a Tattooist

Surrender of a Tattooist

Heart of a Tattooist

Hopes & Dreams of a Tattooist

Tennessee Romance

Whisky Lullaby

Whisky Melody

Whisky Harmony

The Bad Boy Alpha Club

Battle Lines - Part 1

Battle Lines

The Brush Of Love Series

Every Night

Every Day

Every Time

Every Way

Every Touch

The Debt

The Debt: Part 1 - Damn Horse

The Debt: Complete Collection

The University of Gatica Series

The Recruiting Trip

Faster

Higher

Stronger
Dominate
No Rush
University of Gatica - The Complete Series

T.N.T. Series
Troubled Nate Thomas - Part 1
Troubled Nate Thomas - Part 2
Troubled Nate Thomas - Part 3

Undercover Series
Perfect For Me
Perfect For You
Perfect For Us

Unknown Identity Series
Unknown
Unpublished
Unexposed
Unsure
Unwritten
Unknown Identity Box Set: Books #1-3

Unlucky Series
Unlucky in Love
UnWanted

UnLoved Forever

Wet & Wild Series

Stormy Love

Savage Love

Secure Love

Worth It Series

Worth Billions

Worth Every Cent

Worth More Than Money

You & Me - A Bad Boy Romance

Just Me

Touch Me

Kiss Me

Standalone

Wash

Loving Charity

Summer Lovin'

Love & College

Billionaire Heart

First Love

Frisky and Fun Romance Box Collection

Beating Hades' Bikers

Watch for more at www.lexytimms.com.

Bestselling Author

Lexy Timms

when passion meets pleasure...

About the Author

"Love should be something that lasts forever, not is lost forever." Visit USA TODAY BESTSELLING AUTHOR, LEXY TIMMS https://www.facebook.com/SavingForever *Please feel free to connect with me and share your comments. I love connecting with my readers.* Sign up for news and updates and freebies - I like spoiling my readers! http://eepurl.com/9i0vD website: www.lexytimms.com Dealing in Antique Jewelry and hanging out with her awesome hubby and three kids, Lexy Timms loves writing in her free time. MANAGING THE BOSSES is a bestselling 10-part series dipping into the lives of Alex Reid and Jamie Connors. Can a secretary really fall for her billionaire boss?

Read more at www.lexytimms.com.

Made in the USA
Monee, IL
06 January 2026

41171563R00125